NO

LIMIT

www.redbudave.com

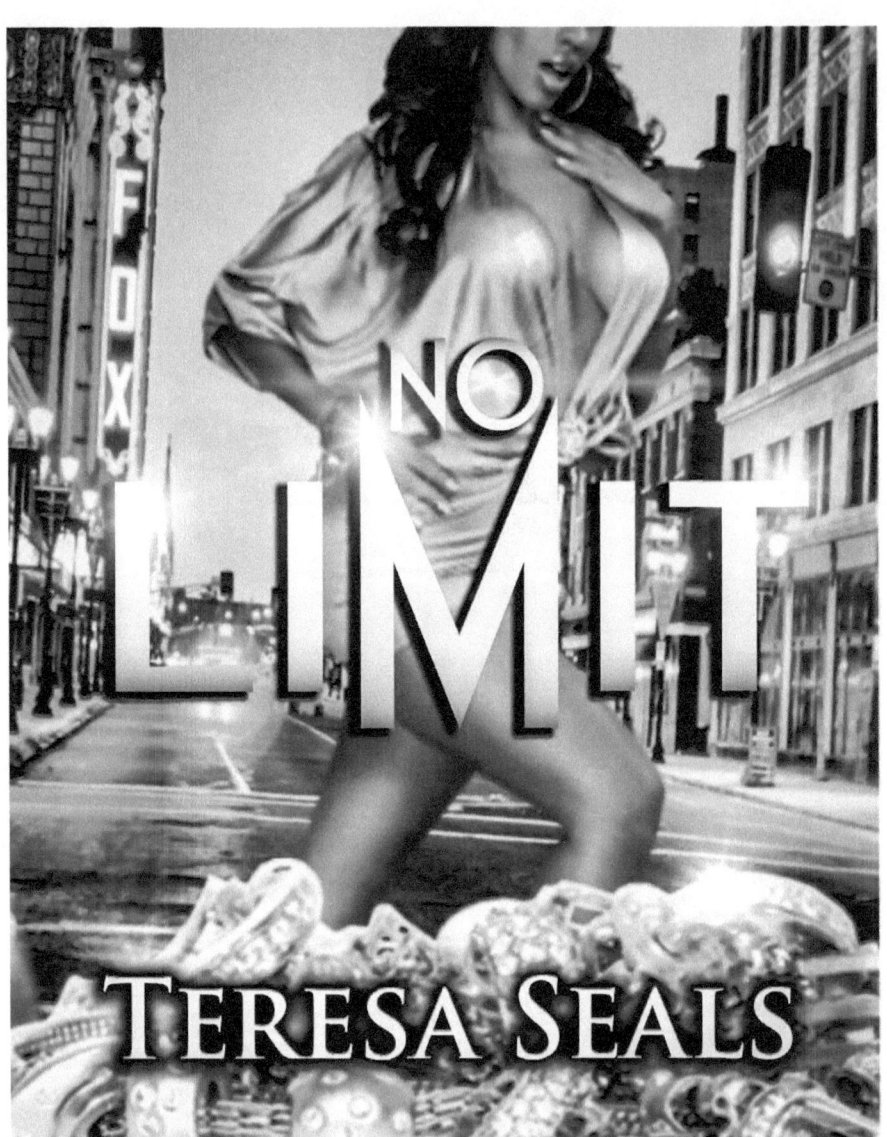

Library of Congress Catalog No.: Pending

ISBN 10: 0-9844397-6-5
ISBN 13: 978-0-9844397-6-8
Cover Design: Robert Ford, Jr.
Editor: Jon B. King

FIRST EDITION

Printed in the United States of America

RED BUD AVE PUBLICATIONS, LLC

Red Bud Ave Publications, LLC is the avenue to that puts your voice in print. Red Bud Ave Publications, LLC is a subsidy publishing company located in St. Louis, MO. Our purpose is to offer those who want to publish their work the assistance in which they will need to get published. Red Bud Ave Publications, LLC serves as the author's professional resource to the author's publishing needs. Please visit www.redbudave.com for more information.

CHECK OUT OTHER TITLES FROM

RED BUD AVE PUBLICATIONS

TAYLOR MADE
SIMPLY TAYLOR MADE
WASHED UP
TALES FROM THE LOU
DIAMONDS ARE TRULY FOREVER (E-book)
MISPLACED LOYALTY

COMING JULY 2017
THE YOUNG AND THE RECKLESS

ACKNOWLEDGMENTS

First and foremost, I want to thank God for blessing me with this gift. I know without Him none of you would be holding this book in your hands. Next up is YOU! Yes, you, I would like to thank you for letting me take up a few hours of your time. Because of people like you, I know that my gift is appreciated. So, I simply want to express my gratitude and appreciation. I know God knows where my journey ends but He has allowed others to watch my journey. Again, I thank you for the support.

Please feel free and email me with your thoughts at booksbyteresaseals@gmail.com

Chapter One

December 12, 2013

Brittany Gates was running, as though she was trying to outdo Usain Bolt, through the terminal of Lambert-St. Louis International Airport with her son Jarvis in tow. She was moving swiftly and Jarvis was keeping up with her as if she were a Kardashian not missing a beat. She could overhear on the airport's intercom, as she got closer to the gate, "C19, last call for flight 5743 to Phoenix," being dispatched for the third time. Brittany was so disgusted with herself that she had sat at the wrong gate for over an hour and a half. She was clinging to their boarding pass as if it was their last supper. When she finally made it to the correct destination, the entire area was empty. There were no patrons waiting to board the next plane. This was unusual. Once an airplane had been boarded and the area was clear; a group of new people would flock to the area to await their time for the next plane that would soon be approaching. All she knew and could remember was her mother telling her that the gate closed ten minutes before the flight departed. The workers need to prepare for take-off. She was there with four minutes to spare. With the entire city looking for her, she knew she couldn't stay in St. Louis one second longer. Missing this flight was not an option for her. When she arrived at gate C19 she immediately handed off each boarding pass to be scanned.

Breathing heavily, Brittany looked down at her son, "Jarvis, you are going to be a track star, just like I was when I was in school, I see!"

She pulled her red St. Louis Cardinals baseball cap tightly over her eyes and looked down at Jarvis as they began to walk through the jet bridge to board the aircraft. Jarvis tugged at his mother shirt to get her attention. She briefly turned around and caught a glimpse of her picture plastered on the television that was hoisted on the wall, near the Chili's restaurant which was directly across from her boarding gate. The airline worker who had just scanned her boarding pass took a glimpse at Brittany and turned her attention back towards the television.

A strange noise abruptly interrupted the dream that Brittany was having. The strange noise startled her. She laid in her bed as though she was paralyzed staring at the ceiling. An odd screeching sound similar to someone's fingernails scratching a chalkboard over and over again, made her turn her head towards her bedroom window. She rose from her stuffed resting position and begin looking at her bedroom door. In the darkness of the room, she felt a slight chill. A small unwanted light from the outside crept into her bedroom through the opened portion of the curtains.

Brittany had to gather herself and her thoughts, she was trying to remember where she was at during that faint moment. In just a few seconds, she realized her whereabouts. She instantly hopped up and ran to Jarvis's bedroom. She stood over Jarvis watching him as he slept peacefully. Not really knowing what her next move would have been if he had not been where she had last seen him, she was just relieved to see her son fast asleep. Then she heard the screeching sound again. Brittany look to the sky and whispered, "Thank you!" She went back to her bedroom walking past her bed and straight towards the bay window. She eased the green satin cover over just enough so that she could peek out.

Brittany giggled to herself as she saw the young girl kneeled down on the side of the gray Impala. She witnessed her married neighbor's side chic keying his car. She had keyed bitch across the hood and swirling loops on the side of which Brittany could see. It was the third time this week she had come by and caused some sort of damage to his car. First, it was all the windows. She even cracked both rear-view mirrors on each side of the car. Second, it was the tires. They were on four flats. When her neighbor, Sean went to have his tires repaired, the guy at the shop let him know there was no physical damage. The air had only been let out each tire.

Brittany chuckled thinking about how time-consuming that was just letting the air out of four tires. She headed towards her nightstand to grab her cell phone. The other day she stood outside with the wife as they were trying to figure out why and who had put all four tires on a flat. She was about to get some evidence of who this car damaging culprit was. Just as she was making her way back to the window with her phone in hand she could hear someone mumbling. She moved slowly wondering with butterflies dancing in her stomach, had Danitra finally caught this chic in the act, she thought. Danitra told Brittany she was going to kill that hoe when she saw her. Danitra didn't seem as though she was mad at the fact her husband was cheating. She was more upset about being embarrassed in front of her neighbors. Mrs. Harris who stayed in the house between Danitra and Brittany had away with looking at you with such disgust. Her evil demonic looks could break down the hardest of the hard. Mrs. Harris would stand on her porch with parched lips and one eyebrow raised high impersonating the St. Louis Arch. You didn't have to wonder about what she was thinking because the intense look let you know what it was. Even if nothing was really wrong, Mrs. Harris had a look that cut like a knife. Her looks were the only thing intimidating but her heart was gold. She was the sweetest and generous person you could have ever met.

Brittany swung the curtain back not caring if she was seen and quickly enough that it may have caught the attention of the two who were outside. She realized that was not a good career move. One tear slowly fell from her left eye as she seen the small frame of the female who was just tagging the Impala fall to the ground on the side of the car.

Brittany stood looking out of her bedroom window in disbelief. Her very own right hand covered mouth as tears began to escape from her hazel eyes and pour down her face. The street light from the lamppost directly across the street had the scene clear as daylight. She could see the blood flowing from the young girl's head. The young girl was now in the darkness of early mid-morning laying in the puddle of her own blood with her eyes wide open. The young girl was gazing as though she was watching her murder's next move and it was nothing she could do to stop him. Her life had been stolen from her and it was nothing she could to do about it to change it. She went from being alone to having being accompanied by an individual who came to seek and destroy. He had accomplished his mission.

Brittany could see the shock that embodied the young girl. Brittany watched as the dread head guy picked the body up and stuffed it in the trunk of her neighbor's gray Impala. Brittany could see the trunk was waiting for this young girl's dead body. It was a clear large piece of plastic covering the entire area. The light from the lamppost gave her a clear view. She didn't have to try to make out what was in the trunk because it could be seen clear as day. As the guy closed the trunk he began to look around. Brittany dropped to her knees and withered on the floor as if she was some sort snaked filled with venom, only her venom was fear. She looked up and noticed her curtain was swaying back and forth. She turned her body back around to reach out to grab it gently so it could stop moving.

Brittany lay on the floor thinking about her aunt saying how she despise when it was hot out. The heat brought the niggas out like dog feces brought flies. *Niggas and flies I despise* would shortly follow as her aunt talked about summertime. What she had just witnessed had Brittany despising the cold weather. Her street was like the city that never slept in the summertime. Someone was always outside no matter the time of day. Even Mrs. Harris was out mean mugging folks in the wee hours of the morning. On this cold December night, not a soul was out. This was one emotional night for Brittany as she fell asleep to the tragedy replaying over and over in her thoughts.

BWEEP BWEEP BWEEP

The sound of Brittany's cell phone's alarm had awakened her. She was still laying in the spot where she had fallen asleep with the crime scene on repeat at two that morning. Brittany kneeled to look out the window. Her car was right behind the Impala but the Impala was no longer there. Both of her neighbors, Sean and Danitra, were standing outside with a city officer from St. Louis Metropolitan Police Department.

Brittany gathered herself and headed down the stairs she had to hear what they were saying first hand. She didn't need to hear second-hand information. Once she reached the door, she waved to her neighbors. She wanted them to see her. Brittany was tempted to walk down there with them. But where they were standing had her shook. They both waved back but the wife began to walk over towards her after she had waved.

"Good morning, Brittany!" Danitra said as she walked up the steps of the porch were Brittany was standing. Danitra tightened the belt to the oversized thick navy blue bathrobe she was wearing with black Ugg boots.

"Hey, Danitra." Brittany said softly, "What's going on?"

"Sean was coming out this morning to leave for work and his car was gone. I've been telling him for years we need to move. We need to be in some secluded area. His only argument is he knows everyone around here and he doesn't have to figure out who's who. Whatever that supposed to mean and then he wants to add the convenience of the highway."

Brittany looked towards her neighbor's house, "I am surprised Mrs. Harris mean ass not outside."

Danitra looked in the same direction, "That is very surprising. She is usually Johnny on the spot. I can't believe her old evil ass not out here."

Brittany chuckled. The main reason she stayed in her family's home was due to the convenience and the one nosey neighbor. The highway was only two minutes away. She could agree with Sean on that about its convenience. Mrs. Harris was an old friend of her grandmother. She would keep an eye on Brittany's mother Pat and aunt Alexis when their mother was at work when they were both young. Her grandmother would always tell her that she was the reason she knew what went on at her house while she was at work. Brittany relied on Mrs. Harris like her grandmother once did. Brittany felt as though Mrs. Harris was her own personal ADT. Any sound or unfamiliar face definitely required a call to 911 in Mrs. Harris's book. Mrs. Harris didn't hesitate or asked any questions she went with her first mind. Mrs. Harris had to be well connected in the department because the police didn't hesitate coming out and to check up on any of her allegations. Brittany got to know the women behind the mask. There was nothing Mrs. Harris wouldn't do for anyone in their time of need. Mrs. Harris had been around long enough to see the changes of the neighborhood. She had witnessed homeowners take pride in the upkeep of their property to renters not caring about a thing. She wasn't afraid of the young generation. Everyone gave her respect. It would be one or two kids they may have mumbled or called her a name. It just wasn't loud enough for Mrs. Harris to hear it. She would come out to make sure none of the neighborhood children walked on her grass. She was the only one of the block whose yard still had its grass. Most yards only had patches and if they did have a full yard filled was grass it was a few patches missing from it. Mrs. Harris's yards was perfectly manicured.

Danitra watched as her husband spoke with the officer and she began her conversation with Brittany, "Did you hear anything last night?"

Brittany had that deer in the headlight look. Brittany was praying Danitra wasn't trying to read her reaction. She looked over towards the officer thinking he may have to save her from Danitra. He was walking in the area where a body had previously fallen. Brittany turned to Danitra, "I didn't see a thing." She felt Danitra looking at her strangely. She pointed at the officer acting as though he was the reason she didn't respond promptly the question, "I wonder what he over there looking for."

"I wonder if that dumb bitch, Leslie is behind this. I believe her ass got keys to his car. I swear once they approve me for this disability check, I am leaving his ass." Danitra said in a matter of a fact tone.

Brittany had heard her leaving him speech all before. Sean had her unemployed tail living the lifestyle of the rich and famous. She had a weekly shopping allowance and their house was plush. When you entered their home you would think you were watching an episode of MTV Cribs. Today Brittany was not about to entertain her or even listen to the spill, "Girl, let me go in here and get ready for work. I am standing here as if I do not have a child to get ready for daycare and I don't have to be at work." Brittany turned to walk in the house.

Danitra began to walk off the porch and right before Brittany closed the door she yelled, "Oh by the way. I read your latest blog. It was so on point. Sean and I had to go to that new spot to check out Comedian Nell Taylor. I must agree with you. There is a lot of unknowns who need big breaks. I know you focus on underground comics and rappers, but I think you should start focusing on authors too in your blogs. I have been reading a lot of good books from people who aren't best sellers. I have to lend you a few of my books." Danitra witnessed Brittany smile with pride as she eased back into her home, "Your grown ass need to give me that onesie!"

Brittany looked down at her black onesie and laughed, "Walmart is waiting on folks to just come there and spend their money for these!" Brittany walked away as if she were the next top model.

Brittany closed the door and walked towards the kitchen. She grabbed the stainless steel tea kettle from the stove and filled it with water. She placed the kettle on the stove and turned the nob on the stove. No flame ignited. She bent down close enough to listen for the ignition and to smell the gas. Nothing happened. So, she tried it again. She gave up, threw the towel down that was in her hand, and walked away. She went back to the front door about to ask Sean if he could come look at her stove. Although he was a janitor at an elementary school, he was also the neighborhood handy man. She was stopped in her tracks as she noticed the white guy headed back to his Laclede Gas work van.

"Damn! They didn't waste any time! I was going to pay the mother fucker today!" Brittany stormed up the steps to wake Jarvis.

Brittany walked into Jarvis's room. He was sound asleep. She didn't want to wake him but it was time. She had wasted twenty minutes of her time standing on the front porch with Danitra. Brittany couldn't understand that whole relationship. Danitra had once worked for EMT as a technician. She was on leave to a lumbar degenerative disc. She claimed it was from lifting heavy individuals who were on the stretcher.

Danitra and Sean had been together for twenty-two years. Neither of them looked over thirty. They were in their late forties. Danitra still had a girlish figure. The only disfigurement were her small sagging titties and Sean still had his boyish young looks. This couple resembled Angela Basset and Michael Ealy. Danitra knew he stepped out but she never seemed as though it bothered her. She only spoke of leaving him but never put it into action.

Brittany woke Jarvis up. He got up out of his bed with no problems as usual. He loved school and wouldn't want to miss a day. She smiled thinking of how he reminded her of her first love. He walked into the bathroom and began to brush his teeth. He then relieved his bladder with the door wide open. Brittany wanted to yell close the door but she decided against it. She never wanted him to hide anything from her the way her younger brother would hide truths from their mother.

"Jarvis, we have to hurry up this morning. I have some important business I need to take care of before I go to work this morning."

"Momma, the water is not getting hot." Jarvis was very intelligent to be four. He paid close attention to tedious details and articulated his thoughts clearly.

Brittany walked towards the bathroom. She thought the little water would at least be warm for the moment. She made it to the sink and tested the water.

"You're right!" She tried to act surprised, "Let's hurry up and get ready. I will call later and find out what's going on."

"Ma, you didn't pay the water bill?" Jarvis asked very seriously.
Brittany looked at him and headed towards her bedroom acting as though he hadn't said anything about a bill.

Brittany was thankful that they always showered and bathed at night. She did her last minute cleaning as she got ready and they were out the door in no time. Brittany dropped Jarvis off at the daycare which was five blocks north of where they lived and was headed to work.

Brittany pulled up at the Check 'N Go. She grabbed her green North Face coat from off the passenger seat. She put it on before she got out the car. She stood on the side of her dark green Mitsubishi Galant and adjusted her jeans.

Brittany walked up to the entrance of the Check 'N Go and waited on one of her home girls to come open the door to the establishment.

Jada came prancing to the door as usual. Brittany chuckled at the fact that she was wearing another Puma jogging suit with her neatly corn rolled extensions. Even though their supervisor, Mark, informed them at their last meeting that they all needed to dress more professional. Jada had let him know it wasn't happening. She told him that they sit behind forty inches of glass and a steel reinforced door all day. Not one customer that came in to pay a bill, cashed a check, wired money or to get a money order worried about what the hell they had on.

"Hey, girl, good morning!" Jada said as she opened the door and locked it back as Brittany entered the threshold.

"Ain't shit good about this morning!" Brittany said dryly as she held back her tears.

Brittany walked through the gray steel door that Jada had left open while Jada stood outside taking her mid-morning smoke break of many. She had been trying to quit. It was so easy for her to walk across the street to the QT to get her fix. Newport's were her choice but she would bum just about any brand. Jada had actually told herself this would be her last day.

"Hey, Crystal and Kierra," Brittany said as she pulled off her coat off and hung it up on the coat rack.

"Why are you so late?" Kierra asked Brittany, noticing she wasn't her high-spirited self.

"Twelve days before Christmas and I am having the roughest morning of my life. I barely got any sleep last night and my mother fucking gas was turned off right when it was time for me to get Jarvis ready for daycare."

Jada came through the door as Brittany was telling about her gas being turned off. Brittany grabbed her cash drawer and placed her calculator, pencil, and paper in her slot. Four windows were available to render service and she sat at the last one, right next to Crystal.

Ten minutes before the establishment opened, Kierra started with their brief morning meeting. She was the supervisor on site during their shift. Their store had only two shifts. It was the only store of the four that wasn't twenty-four hours. Their general supervisor Mark had four other sites. He would stop in at least three times during the week to meet the Brinks guy when he did his weekly pick-ups and drop-offs. She let them know that the cash on hand was only close to ten grand. That was low for this site. They easily maintained a million dollars. There was over seventy-five business in the vicinity and the community had a population over twenty thousand. The demographics of the Check 'N Go called for them to have an abundant amount of cash on hand but this day was different.

"Hopefully today we only do wire transfers, money orders, and bill pay. You know we are usually slow on Wednesdays." Kierra said as she sat in her seat which was the first by the steel door.

It was no now opening time. Eight o'clock came so fast. Jada went to unlock the door. She paused as she seen the officer parked behind Brittany's car. While she stood there she pulled out another cigarette. She quickly threw it down when she saw the tow truck pull up five minutes later. She ran over to Brittany's car.

"What the fuck are y'all doing?" Jada stood in front of the car so the tow truck driver couldn't hitch Brittany's car to his tow truck.

The officer looked Jada over and chuckled. Standing four eleven and weighing an average of 130 he knew it wasn't much harm she could cause, "Ma'am, is this your car?" the officer asked.

"I wouldn't be asking what hell you all are doing if it wasn't!" Jada said in her matter of the fact tone.

The officer smiled exposing his pearly whites, "I am going to have to write you a ticket for improper plates, expired tags, and a slew of parking tickets."

Jada thought about being arrested. She loved Brittany dearly but she wasn't about to do her time. Not over some parking tickets anyway. She moved out of their way, "Sir, sorry for interrupting. This is not my car. That's my car over there." She pointed to a random car and turned to walk back into her job. She disappeared from the scene as fast as she appeared.

When Kierra was done with her customer she opened the door for Jada so that she could enter. Kierra and Jada made eye contact but didn't say anything. Kierra watched as Jada walked over to Brittany. Jada said a few words and Brittany just shook her head.

From where Crystal was sitting she and Brittany could barely see what was going on outside with Brittany's car. What they could see was Brittany's car hitched up off the ground and slowly being dragged away.

"I was just waiting to file my taxes. I was going to take care of everything with that damn car as soon as I cashed the check." Brittany said as she held back the tears.

Jada chuckled, "B, you don't have to worry. You know I am here for you and my godson. I will just be your personal chauffer until you get things straight. Unless you wanna just go steal your car!" Jada swayed over to her seat.

"Fuck getting things straight! We could set this bitch off come the first of the month and we will all be straight! You know that it will be three to four million dollars in this camp during the first and fifteenth of the month?" Crystal yelled.

Brittany looked at Kierra as she shook her head in agreement. They both were disgusted with Crystal and found her comment ridiculous. Then they both looked back at Crystal.

Jada looked them all over, "Shit that doesn't sound like a bad idea! We can split that money four ways. How much would we each get if its four million dollars?"

Brittany looked at Crystal as she ignored Jada, "See just stupid! It's four of us and it would be four million dollars. Do the math! You can't blame not knowing how to divide on Common Core because it didn't exist when we were in school. I am getting ready to pay my damn gas bill. Jada, when we get off you can take me to go get Jarvis and you can take us home. And, maybe I'll let Jarvis tutor you for a minute." Brittany laughed.

"B, you need to get down with this plan. You hurting for money. Hell, we all hurting for money. We can do this so sweet and don't have to be worried about nothing for a minute." Jada said trying to convince Brittany.

"You're exactly right. For a minute. If I steal anything, I don't want worry about nothing for the rest of my life." Brittany turned to

Crystal, "Frankie, and this little Stoney reject can get the fuck outta my face. I ain't robbing or blowing up a thing. Furthermore, y'all need to stop smoking that shit! It's frying all y'all little brain cells!"

A few customers entered and ended their conversation. Brittany worked a few customers and stepped towards the back door with her debit card to call and make her payment for her gas bill. The check cashing place became so busy with patrons doing money orders and bill paying, their shift was over before they knew it. Five o'clock had come so fast. The second shift that closed the store at one in the morning was starting to enter. They did their shift change and was able to clock out. Jada did as she said and was taking Brittany to get Jarvis and then home.

As they turned on Brittany's street the fire trucks and several police cars had the street blocked off. Brittany sat there confused for a few seconds. Then she jumped out of the car. She made it half way down the street and Danitra stopped her. Brittany fell in Danitra's arms. She couldn't believe that her home and burned completely down. They frame looked like old charcoal on a barbecue pit.

Brittany remembered leaving the towel on the stove that she never turned off when she went to the door to get Sean to see why the stove hadn't turned on.

Teresa Seals

Chapter Two

May 15, 2008

Brittany stood in the mirror smiling like a Cheshire cat admiring her hazel eyes and flawless caramel skin. She was impressed with her friend's Crystal skills. Never attending a beauty school, a day in her life but she could do some hair. She had magic hands and any head she touched became automatically fly. A gene she had to inherit from her mother, Crystal had the magic touch. Brittany adjusted her gold graduation cap on her head. With her left hand, she moved the tassel from the right side to the left side. Her mother, Pat, stood there proudly. She was smiling as if she had done all the hard work to get Brittany to that point where she was about to walk across the stage as a graduate of class 2008.

Pat entered the bathroom with Brittany and kissed her on her cheek. She removed the graduation cap from Brittany's head and picked up the flat iron.

"Your Bob looks good, but it needs a tight bump in the back. It has lost the small curl in the back. It's like it's hanging straight. Crystal really needs to being trying to her cosmetology license. I have to admit she has skills." Pat said as she fixed her hair.

Brittany's eyes glistened as she smiled admiring her fat nose, "Crystal did do her thang but it's all me anyway. You know when this is all over I am just going to pull it back into a ponytail." Brittany laughed.

Pat combed through her hair, "Brittany, I couldn't wait for this day to come. Ever since you were a little girl I couldn't wait for this day. I thought I was going to have to put off my relocation for another year but the looks of it, Brandon, will not be graduating. So, my flight is booked for tomorrow. I will only be returning briefly to help you with this." Pat said as she put the comb down and patted Brittany on her pregnant belly.

Brandon barged right in, "Excuse me, ladies, I do have a graduation to prepare for."

Pat and Brittany moved out of Brandon's way as he barged in the bathroom as though they were not standing there in the first place. It was a smooth transition even with his rudeness and now the ladies began to observe Brandon from the hallway.

"What fragrance is that you are wearing?" Pat looked Brandon directly in his eyes expecting him to lie.

"Pat, I am not wearing a fragrance. I just got done smoking this fat ass blunt and I want you to know that you are not about to blow my high. I am about to close this door and shower so I can be ready in three hours for my sister's graduation." Brandon slammed the door in Pat's face.

Pat wasn't pleased with disrespect her youngest child displayed. She wanted to react but she knew he was angry about the past. She loved him dearly and she wanted to blow up and retort. A part of her wanted to let him know that she would no longer tolerate his impudence and it would be the last time he behaved in that manner towards her. Pat decided against it.

Brittany walked to her room and closed her door. She knew things had just hit the fan. She didn't want to watch Pat has she pitched a fit with her brother. She knew it was about to pop off as she watched from the distance. Brandon was standing there talking to their mother with his chest out. He stood there like he was the man of the house who was addressing his wife after he had paid all the bills. In this case, Brandon hadn't paid a thing and he was being the defiant child he was known to be. She did not want her big day ruined. She walked into her room and closed her door. Even though Pat would be screaming at a close door, she didn't want to hear the bickering that was bound to take place. Brittany grabbed her headphones and slid them on and laid across her bed. She drifted off to sleep listening to Alicia Keys *As I Am* cd.

"Excuse me, Mrs. Neal, can you send Brittany Gates to the counselor's office?" the principal's secretary said over the intercom.

Brittany's 5th-grade teacher, Mrs. Neal, nodded her head in her direction signaling her approval to follow the instructions, "She's on her way down now."

Before Brittany left the classroom she scanned the room to look at her friends. She was praying that they could walk this mile with her. She locked eyes with Jada. She was watching as though she was about to break out and cry. Brittany couldn't take her eyes of Jada and Jada eyes were locked on Brittany. She almost ran towards the door as her friend was exiting the room. Jada had a look of confusion displayed on her face. She kept her eyes fixed on Brittany until she couldn't see her anymore. She didn't look at Crystal and Kierra. She knew they were watching her. The three of them together was fighting an evitable force. They all wanted to get up out of their seats and go after their friend. They knew Mrs. Neal was not having it so they all just dazed at the door. None of them knew what Brittany was going to the principal's office for but it couldn't have been a good thing. The call came out of nowhere. As far as they were concerned, their day school day had come to an end. There was no work getting completed until their friend returned back to class. In the very beginning, they all grew with concerned without a valid reason.

All four girls met in kindergarten. They somehow managed to go from kindergarten to fifth grade in the same classroom together. Over the years their bond grew stronger and the remained close friends.

Jada was an only child. She lived with her grandparents and her mother when she wasn't on one of her extended vacations. Her mother kept Jada in the latest fashions. Her mother's line of work didn't provide a stable home environment but it kept her closet filled with the latest designers.

Crystal was the youngest of three girls who came from a two-parent home. She and her siblings, which were twins were ten years apart. Crystal dad was the breadwinner. During the day her father drove for a local company that provided all the nick-nacks that the corner stores throughout the city were supplied with. By night his was the neighborhood supplier off all things from things socks, washing powder, and CDs. Whatever you needed he could get his hands on it. He even got rid of Jada's mother merchandise every once in a while. His biggest side hustle was during the summer. He was known throughout the city as the fireworks man.

Crystal's mother was a beautician. She had a select few of clients. That's because she worked from the house. She didn't want too many people coming to where she lay her head. Back in the day, long before Crystal came along, she had her own shop, The Hair Clinic. One of the major players in St. Louis bought her very own beauty shop. Everything was seized when he was arrested. He believed on of his friends was behind the dismantling of his lucrative lifestyle. His close friend was in the same circle. He had owned laundromats, car washes, and a few lounges. None of his assets were seized. Crystal's mother and her older twin sisters were left homeless. They slept in the only thing that wasn't seized during the process.

The only thing her mother had in her name and was able to prove that her revenue from doing hair purchased her 1987 300E four doors, Mercedes-Benz. Her mother vowed never to mess with another street guy. If it hadn't been for Crystal's father she didn't know how long she and the twins would have had to sleep in the Benz. He would come in her shop daily to sell odds and in. When he came in he would flirt with her and tell her one day she was going to be his lady. That day eventually came.

Kierra was Crystal's cousin. They were brother's daughters. Kierra's parents were heroin users. Crystal's parents had taken Kierra when she was three years old. Crystal's dad was forty and her mother was thirty-eight when she was born. Her mom convinced her dad to take Kierra in so that Crystal would always have someone to keep her company. She would let him know daily how her twins entertained each other and barely bothered her. She would take them to the park and watch them play. All she did was clothed, feed them and spent a few minutes on disciplining them every now and then. She went on to say she talked about the facts of life on occasion. He agreed. Although the girls knew that they were cousins, they were raised more like sisters.

Brittany made it to the counselor's office. She was taken back when she reached the door. She was trying to make out just what was going on. She couldn't speak. Brittany scanned the room. There were only two faces out of the four people sitting in an office that she recognized. Her brother Brandon and the school counselor that came in her classroom once a week to talk about careers. Brittany looked at her little brother as he sat between a strange Caucasian woman dressed in a gray pantsuit looking like Hillary Clinton with her hair pinned up in a bun on the top of her head and a black officer that didn't look older than Jada's older sisters.

Ms. Mallory, the school counselor, began to introduce everyone in the room. The entire time she was talking. Brittany kept her eyes directly on Brandon. She could only imagine what he had told those people. She was trying to smile to keep from crying. Her thoughts were interrupted as she could hear Ms. Mallory asking did she know where her mother worked. Brittany took her eyes off Brandon for a second to look at Ms. Mallory. Brittany was not about to tell anyone where her mother worked. Her closest friends didn't know where her mother worked. She loved her mother dearly but she was embarrassed by her line of work.

She looked at Brandon and tried to choose her words carefully. The only thing that rolled off her tongue was, "You little rat!" Then she leaned in to charge him. The officer stopped her in mid-air. Ms. Mallory stood from her desk and instructed Brittany to have a seat at her desk.

The caseworker had stated why she was there and what was about to happen. Brittany was in disbelief. Just last week she was supporting her mother, who had just buried her mother, and now this. Even though her mother was never home at night, she always waited until her children were sleep before she left. She and her brother were always with their grandmother up until she became sick and was placed in a nursing home.

Brittany sat in disbelief as she listened to how their mother was a prostitute. Strange women and men entered their house every night. The women were allowed to have sex with Brandon and the men were allowed to have sex with Brittany. Brittany sat listening to this story Brandon had fabricated that was about to have them removed from their mother and their home. Brandon had only told this story to prevent from getting suspended for the eighth time this school year and it was only the beginning of October and the school had just started the end of August.

Pat was an exotic dancer. She never brought anyone to their house. When Pat was contacted by the caseworker, she informed her of the matter. She let her know that they would be placed in a group home her while the investigation took place. They had to make sure that the children were not being sexually exploited. The way Brandon and Brittany rocked, Pat assumed that this was something they conjured up together. She would question the love her children had for her. They had spent a lot of time with her mother and she wondered if they were upset with her for not being the mother her mother had been to her children.

For six years, Brandon and Brittany's residence was Every Child's Hope Children's Home. Pat didn't attend a court date and she stopped answering the caseworker calls. Pat had just lost her mother and now she had lost her children. The only other person she considered family was her sister Alexis. Alexis and Pat had a love-hate relationship. There was a ten-year difference between the two. Pat loved her because she was her little sister. She just hated sharing their mother. Alexis didn't like the fact their mother was stern with her and lenient with Alexis.

Brittany and Brandon were able to continue to attend school in the same district. This helped Brittany get through this heart-rending time. She was never separated from Jada, Crystal, and Kierra. Brandon, on the other hand, had a rough transition. He never expected that his little get out trouble free card would land him in a group home. The boys tortured him for being a little pretty boy with hazel eyes and curly hair. One day he was fed up. Kevin, the leader of the torture was getting ready to start. He walked up behind Brandon and gave him a wedgie. Brandon full of rage turned with his visible wedgie and beat Kevin with his bare hands. Kevin, light as day with sandy red hair had two black eyes to accompany his dusty look. The remainder of his stay was peaceful. After that fight, not one boy bothered him at all. The workers were glad that day came. Brandon did what they wanted to do. He thought Brittany would hate him. In the beginning, she did, but as time passed she became more pissed at Pat. Brandon was so pissed with her and it never changed. He knew he had down wrong but his mother even tried to find out why. Brandon was missing his nanna Lillie. He knew her love could never be replaced.

24

The beginning of Brittany's junior year of high school Pat began to work on getting her children back. Pat had changed her lifestyle. She stops working at the strip club and found her full-time job. During an annual exam, she was informed that she had small fibroid tumors. The doctor informed her that in was nothing to be concerned about at that moment. If she didn't get them removed she would later need to become a concern. She thought six years was long enough time where her children should have learned their lesson.

Pat thought it would be a good idea to make amends with her children. She had gotten hired as a Ramp Agent with Southwest Airlines. Within six months of employment, she became a Grounds Operations Supervisor. When they let her know that she may need to relocate to Phoenix, Arizona, she figured she could stop living the single kid-free life.

Brittany was happy to be back home with her mother. She knew that she wouldn't have long before she was about to graduate from high school and be off to colleges. Brandon, on the other hand, was not that excited about Pat's return. He held a grudge and didn't let it go. He never felt that her abandoning them should be a long-term punishment. Brandon lied and she didn't even care to know why.

Brandon barged into Brittany's room. He stood over his sister watching her as she lay in the bed with her headphones. He tapped her on her arm, "B, it's almost time to go. What are you not going to your graduation? Jada just pulled up." Brandon rumbled.

Brittany opened her eyes and just stared at Brandon. He was just a blur in the beginning. Brittany rubbed her eyes, raised up and removed her headphones.

"You need to quit tripping with Pat. That was all your fault. Everything!" Brittany said to her brother.

Brandon held up his hands. He displayed five fingers on one hand and one finger on the other. In a split second, he was holding up his middle finger on both hands. He let out, "Her," as he wiggled his middle fingers back and forth in Brittany's face. He then followed Brittany as she walked out of her room headed to meet her friend Jada.

Teresa Seals

Chapter Three

You have a collect call from, Jarvis. An inmate in Southeast Correctional facility. This call is subject to be recorded. To accept the charges, dial eight. To deny the charges dial nine.

Brittany pressed the number eight on her cell phone. She smiled as she envisioned her chocolate drop. He stood six foot even. Jarvis always rocked the Lil Boosie fade since the day she met him. He was very charismatic and possessed a mesmerizing deep seductive voice. Brittany thought he resembled Idris Elba and had the swag of T.I.

"Hey, baby. How you and my son are doing?" Jarvis asked in a rhythmic tone.

"It's all bad. I've had a rough few days." Brittany responded.

"You wanna switch places?" Jarvis joked.

"At this point, I would," Brittany spoke with a dry tone.

Jarvis could hear in her voice something was wrong, "Where are you?"

"Right now I am sitting in Jada's car about to go into the post office to turn in my change of address," Brittany informed Jarvis.

Brittany filled Jarvis in with the turn of events that she had undergone the past few days. Jarvis became upset with himself because he was not on the streets to fend for his family. He had missed the birth of his child, his graduation, and now he was missing out on being the support team Brittany needed.

Jarvis thought about the day he was arrested and picked out of the lineup. He and his brother Jarvon looked so much alike that he and Jarvis were often mistaken for one another. Jarvon had snatched a woman's purse as she exited the Chinese restaurant. He hopped in a silver F150 he had recently stolen and sped off. The women picked Jarvis in the lineup. The F150 belong to a police officer. The F150 had been used in a dozen robberies throughout the city in a matter of four days.

Jarvis had driven the truck to see Brittany. On his way back home, as he was about to turn onto his street, five police cars had swarmed him. Jarvis knew his brother stole cars but he didn't think this truck was stolen. It was the first vehicle that he had with keys. He found out that Jarvon took the truck from an off-duty cop at gunpoint. The cop had left his department-issued Glock 17 in his vehicle.

When Jarvon was arrested and sentence a year after Jarvis, he regretted the decision he made. He figured if he wanted to go to jail he could have been doing his on the bid in the first place. Jarvis had to stop thinking about it before he became upset. He didn't want to do that because he would only wind up in the hole. The place he spent his first three years of being incarcerated.

Jarvis and Jarvon's parents were so upset with their sons. They had worked so hard to provide them with a different lifestyle. Their parents had planned things so precisely. They married young, enjoyed each other and traveled the world. They were in their late thirties when their children were born. Jarvis and Jarvon mother was a licensed agent with a fortune five hundred insurance company. She was the first black female to reach the plateau of having nearly a thousands of people to purchase life insurance and invest in their retirement. His dad worked for American Multinational Corporation that designed, manufactured, marketed, and distributed vehicles and vehicle parts, and sold financial services since he had graduated from his high school. Janice and Jacob had done well for themselves but their children were doing just the opposite. Well one of them anyway.

Once Jarvis was off the phone, Brittany went into the post office. She needed to change her address to Jada's place of residence. She didn't know how long she would need to stay with Jada but she needed to make sure she received all the important documents or any other mail. When she made it out the post office she needed to call Brandon and her mom.

Brandon and his girlfriend, Demeasha, had moved into their apartment in Canfield Green Apartments. When Brandon found out Demeasha was pregnant he enrolled in a GED program and found employment through a temp service. When Brandon passed his GED he didn't stop there. He enrolled at Ranken Technical College.

At Ranken, he focused on Construction and Heating and Cooling. Demeasha's due date was February 14th. In December she was placed on bedrest. Brittany was proud of her little brother. He was standing on his feet as the man he tried to be at Pat's house.

Brittany called Brandon to let him know what had happened to their family's home. One part of Brandon was disappointed and the other was relieved. He thought about the precious moments he spent with his grandmother. He was longing for one of her stories and all the meals she prepared with love. The yearning for some of her fried chicken grew stronger. Another part of him was glad that the memories he had of Pat were going up in smoke. He opened his door to his home for Brittany and Jarvis. Brittany declined. She didn't know much about Demeasha and she wasn't trying to get to know her under those type of circumstances.

Pat didn't take it as well as Brandon. She was upset that her mother's house was no longer. She thought about all the keepsakes that she left behind, that were in the basement, were destroyed. She let Brittany know with the insurance she could rebuild but that wouldn't replace the memories. While listening to Pat, Brittany realized just how selfish her mom really was. The entire time she complained about what was damaged and she couldn't retrieve; she never asked how she was doing or where she and Jarvis were going to stay. Brittany wanted to ask her mom for the money to get her car out the tow yard. She decided against it. When her mother took a break from talking, Brittany just ended the call. She shook it off and was headed to work. Pat called back and Brittany sent her straight to voicemail.

Brittany realized she needed to call one more person. She needed to call Pat's older sister, Alexis. All while Brittany and Brandon were awarded to the state, Alexis made sure she visited them twice a month. She would let them know how their mother was doing and how betrayed she felt about the false accusations. Alexis would let Brittany know that she wouldn't go against her sister wishes. That's why she wasn't fighting to remove them from the group home. She felt bad for visiting because Pat wanted them to suffer. Alexis couldn't find it in her heart to just leave them for dead.

They had a very complicated situation. Right, when Pat was in the process of working on getting them back, the children's home was on the verge of closing. Several foster children were about to be displaced or returned to a terrible situation. The only place available was the juvenile detention center and they were about to be overcrowded like a state penitentiary.

"Hey, Aunt Alexis."

"Hey, Brittany." Alexis smiled just from hearing Brittany's voice. Although Alexis didn't have any children, Brittany and Brandon filled the void. At times people would think that her niece and nephew were her very own children as much time as she spent talking about them. When in Alexis looked at Brittany's caramel flawless skin, high

31

cheekbones, slanted hazel eyes and shoulder length thick dark brown hair, she saw a youthful Pat and Alexis.

"Auntie, I have some very bad news," Brittany spoke softly.

"Gone spill it!" Alexis sat down on her bed.

"Grandma's house caught fire." Brittany waited for her aunt to ask her what had happened.

"What nigga were you fooling around with that has set the house on fire? Boy, I tell you. *Niggas and flies I so despise!*" Alexis shook her head and was trying to hold back the tears. She knew Pat kept up with all the insurance and taxes so she wasn't worried about repairs.

"Well Auntie it's sort of my fault," Brittany continued so her aunt wouldn't interrupt, "The gas was off and I didn't know. I turned the stove on and walked away. Well before I walked away, I placed the dish rag down on the stove. When I got to work, I paid the bill. My services were restored and…" Brittany couldn't finish. Pat had cut her off.

"Awe, baby girl, I am sorry. I know you are a nervous wreck. You know you and Jarvis are welcome to come here until you get you alls housing situation straight." Pat was about to ask her did she call her mother. She decided against it. She knew her sister was selfish and probably thought of herself during the process.

Brittany broke down crying. She had been holding back those tears for years. Her aunt had just said what she wanted her mother to say. She didn't care that her mother was in Phoenix, Arizona. She just wanted her to extend the offer. Brittany let her know she appreciated the offer and they were staying with Jada. She even went on to tell her aunt about her car. Her aunt let her know she didn't have to worry about transportation. She would help her get her car back.

Brittany's aunt wasn't considered as wealthy but she had a few coins. She worked at a company called Boeing as a Materials, Process & Physics engineer. Boeing is the world's largest aerospace company. She had worked at Boeing ever since she had graduated from high school. She started off as a temp that just logged and scanned in airplane parts. While working there, she enrolled in college and majored in physics. This led her to make the top dollars. She was two years shy of retiring.

Alexis told Brittany to find out how much she needed to take care of her car and call her back with the amount. Brittany let her know when she got to work she would do it. Before she got off the phone, Alexis let her know that she could just go get her a car. Brittany let her know that she was still paying a car note and she only had five payments left. She didn't a repossession reflected on her credit report. Alexis let her know that she understood and that she would be waiting for her phone call.

Chapter Four

Brittany, Jarvis, and Jada entered the laundromat. Brittany paused blocking the doorway as she saw a familiar face on the television screen. She swiftly moved towards the television and looked up to read the caption. The T.V. was on but the volume had to be on mute. Brittany's eyes were glued to the screen. She couldn't hear a sound but she knew exactly what the reporter was speaking about. The fresh smell of flowery detergents and the sounds of items bonking the glass on the dryers couldn't interrupt her thoughts. She walked away with the image and the words displayed on the screen about Leslie Collins had been missing for five days.

Jada watched Brittany as she walked to the washing machine where she was putting her clothes. "You know that girl?" Jada looked at Brittany waiting on her to respond.

Brittany never looked up, "No, I don't know her. I thought she looked familiar."

Jada watched Brittany's body language. She was confused and wanted to know why she was shaking. For a minute, Jada thought she Brittany was behind her disappearance. They had been together so long that they knew some of the same people. Jada didn't know what was going on but Brittany displayed that something was going on. She was going to get to the bottom of this one way or another. Jada just had to find out how.

Brittany looked at Jada, "That's crazy. Right here at Christmas. I thought my situation was bad but a family is mourning a loss of their loved one."

Jada with a frown on her face turned towards Brittany, "Girl, that girl has been missing. Where have you been? She has been on the news every day. How is a family mourning a loss? She may return! Hell, niggas die every day. Folks don't get numb over deaths anymore. Murders, homicides, and manslaughter is becoming just as normal as washing your ass." Jada searched for some sort of sign as she waited on Brittany to say more.

Brittany slowly let the top to the washing machine down, "I guess you are unaware of all that human trafficking taking place. That girl is not about to turn up." Brittany was not about to tell her friend that she saw as Leslie Collins lost her life and she knew for a fact that her body was not about to turn up. Brittany knew she had to pull it together. She was becoming uncomfortable and she knew Jada was recognizing her discomfort. Brittany took a deep breath and walked away from Jada. She couldn't go to sleep at night thinking about the shocked look Leslie Collins had as she lay on the ground outside of Brittany's bedroom window.

Jada chuckled and spoke loud enough so that Brittany could hear her, "You know little Betsey Bruce, human trafficking could be a good topic you could put on your little blog. I know those million followers you have would rather read about that more than those boring blogs about unknown comedians and underground rap artist."

Brittany laughed at Jada as she compared her to well-known news anchor in the St. Louis area with over forty-five years appearing on the local news. Little did Jada know that those comedians and underground rap artist were the reason she had a million followers. Writing those boring blogs as Jada called them were special to the individuals she wrote about and the people who supported them.

Those unknowns help grow her audience. She didn't care what Jada had to say or how she felt about what she discussed on her blog.

"My next boring blog will be about you and the day you finally open that boutique you being talking about since we graduated high school." Brittany gained her composure. She hated when her friends tried to downplay her dream. She waited on Jada to respond. Brittany was ready to tell Jada all about how she just talked a good game about fashion but wasn't going to do anything about it to contribute to the industry.

"Here you go sounding like Crystal. Go ahead and ask me why I want to open a boutique and everybody's doing it?" Jada said very sarcastically.

They were on opposite sides of the laundromat. In the beginning, other customers were tuned in looking as though they were waiting for something to pop off. They quickly went back to folding their clothes and looking in their cell phones when they noticed it was just a mere discussion taking place.

"I am not about to knock your dream. I guess when Crystal goes to beauty school and Kierra enrolled in her real estate classes; you might just be opening your boutique. Just cause everybody and they momma opening boutiques, yours is going to be different. Plus, you will have a million plus people that will know all about your endeavors. So, you can thank me and my boring blog now." Brittany smirked and blew Jada a kiss. She wants to remain the loyal friend that uplifted, inspired and motivated her crew to do better.

"Aunt J, can I have some more quarters for the video game?" Jarvis asked Jada.

Jada walked over to the change machine with Jarvis in tow. She slid a five-dollar bill inside and retrieved the quarters. She gave Jarvis four quarters and he ran off.

Jada slowly watched Brittany as she watched a dread head guy as he entered the laundromat. Jada was thinking to herself how Brittany loved a nice piece of chocolate. Today was different. She didn't display a lustful look at that moment she looked to be startled. Jada got all in Brittany's face, "B, what's up? You look like you seen a ghost." Brittany was not herself since the dread had individual entered the laundromat. Her disposition was throwing Jada. They were now sitting next to each other scrolling through their phones. Brittany looked up every few seconds to make sure Jarvis was still playing the game and seeing what the dread head guy was doing. She slid her phone into her pocket and just watched Jarvis from the distance.

Brittany jumped, "I was just thinking. I need to call Danitra and see how she is doing." Brittany reached toward her back pocket and pulled out her phone. She put Danitra's name into her search engine and pressed to call her when the number popped up. She watched the guy as he placed his clothes in the washer. Brittany was about to take her clothes out but Danitra answered the phone.

"Hey, Danitra! What's going on? I've been meaning to call you." Brittany waited on Danitra to speak.

"Girl, I gotta call you back. Something is going on inside Mrs. Harris's house. It's all kind of police out here. It's too cold out here to be holding a phone. I'll call you when I get in the house." Danitra hung up the phone.

Brittany tried not panic but the guy she saw kill Leslie Collins was in the laundromat with her. She knew she couldn't tell Jada. She tried to act as normal as possible. She took her clothes out the washer and placed them in the rolling cart. She wheeled the object over to the dryers. She made three more trips to the dryers and went to have a seat where Jarvis was playing Mrs. Pac-Man. She could see the murderer in her peripheral so she kept him in her view.

She watched as he walked outside and reentered with his clothing items. She was a little at ease when she noticed that he was there to do his laundry. She figured she wouldn't be as obvious to the other women who were gawking him.

Chapter Five

Jada lay across her couch in peace. She was glad she had her apartment to herself. Brittany and Jarvis had gone out to eat with Brittany's aunt Alexis. Jada didn't want to admit but she was missing chauffeuring Brittany around. She grabbed her IPad and her little notebook. She had been doing her research on suppliers and tips to open up *Pink Legacy Boutique*. She had a love for fashion and she wanted to share it with the world. Her mother had dreams of establishing her own clothing line. She once wanted to be like Chanel but she was too caught up in the thrill she had from stealing fashions. Jada embraced her mother's passion. She googled, read and took notes. She was three hours in when Crystal had called her.

Jada went to scan her closet. What could she throw on to go hang out she thought to herself. She opted for a hot pink ruffle sleeveless blouse and some jeans she had ripped and placed a pattern of hot pink roses that peaked out through the rips. She was having a time with the shoes. Once she decided that she was going to put on her tan leather jacket. She knew her tan leather wedged Ugg boots would complete her outfit. She walked into her bathroom and looked at herself. She knew it was time to take her braids down. She had them for Christmas and she wasn't about to bring the New Year in with them. Jada needed to get with Crystal so she could get some fresh braids. She grabbed the hair mousse to lay the frizz down and placed a scarf on her head so that she could jump in the shower.

Jada admired her naked tight petite frame. She grabbed her Victoria's Secret lotion. Pure Seduction was a favorite fragrance. She opened the top and prepared to rub lotion on her Mocha skin tone. She would glance in the mirror that hung from the back of her bedroom door admiring her body.

Jada dressed and posed in the mirror admiring herself. She took the scarf off and took another look. "Even with raggedy braids, Will Smith would still love this Jada." She blew herself a kiss and headed to the door. She thought about going to visit her grandparents but she met up with Crystal. She knew they were probably just sitting in their living room watching the Game Show network. They were getting up in age. They spent the majority of their time in front the television and visiting their incarcerated daughter while Jada was just living her young life.

She was startled when she saw her friend from the laundromat standing at the door. "Bryson, what are you doing? Why didn't you call?" Jada didn't notice the pink roses and bottle of Freaky Moscato he was holding in his hands.

"My dreads need to be re-twisted. I thought that we could chill and get twisted." Bryson smiled.

"First of all," Jada moved to the outside and Bryson stepped back giving her space. She closed the door behind her and spoke loud enough in the hallway so her nosey neighbors could hear her, "My friend lives here with me, so you can't just be popping up at my place of residence. Secondly, I don't do pop up visits. When and if I do invite you over will be the only time you are allowed in my home!"

"Alright, lil feisty momma. My bad! I got it. Don't come until ask too!" Bryson laughed, "Can I walk you to your car since it looks like you are about to leave?"

Jada looked him over. She couldn't believe that the guy she met four days ago was standing outside her door. She was trying to remember if she had even told him where she stayed. She couldn't remember what she said during the late nights she spent caking with him on the phone. "No, I don't mind. With all those muscles, I know you can keep me safe." Jada rubbed her hand over his muscular arm as they exited her apartment building.

Jada was looking for a parking space. She knew she should have just ridden with Crystal and Kierra. Right as she circled the block for the fourth time she saw a car about to leave. She stopped her car and cut on her blinker waiting for the car to pull out. She didn't like going anywhere in downtown St. Louis. She could never find parking. Kierra had a thing for jazz and like to frequent the club Jazz at the Bistro nightclub.

Jada looked up in her review mirror, "Go around stupid motherfucka!" Jada was talking like the individual in the black Monte Carlo could hear her. The car sped around her almost hitting the car she was waiting to pull out of the parking space she was waiting on to pull into the park. Jada saw what look like some dreads. For a minute, she thought it was Bryson. She laughed. "Just about everybody in the Lou rocking locks." She said aloud as she tried to remember if there was a black Monte Carlo on her parking lot at her complex. She couldn't remember. Bryson stood and watched her as she pulled off. She was about to call him and decided against it when Kierra hit her window.

"Girl, we about to go to the Broadway. So follow us." Kierra said as she and Crystal were headed to Crystal's car."

Jada held her head out the window of her car, "Can we go get something to eat first. I haven't eaten all day!"

Crystal pulled out her cell phone to call Jada, "Do you want to drive thru or sit down?"

"Girl, when have you known me to drive thru anyplace? I wanna sit down." Jada said in her matter of a fact tone.

"Keep in mind we are going to the Broadway in North County so think of something to eat in that area. Well, you lead and we will follow." Crystal ended the call.

Jada actually had taste for Red Lobster but she knew that they were bound to complain. She led them to Applebee's Grill & Bar.

They pulled on Applebee's parking lot and parked right next to each other.

"Seriously, club Applebee's?" Kierra said with sarcasm in her tone.

This was the one Applebee's' that was always crunk like a nightclub. They waited approximately fifteen minutes to before they were escorted to their seats. They had perfect timing because usually, the wait on a Saturday night would have roughly been around thirty minutes or longer. Why they were waiting for Jada had to fill them in on her little run in with Bryson. She actually had to start from the beginning on how they met and bring them up to date. She was keeping him a secret for some strange reason. She thought that Brittany was checking him out for a minute but she knew that wasn't the case. The only person Brittany was worried about was Jarvis. She had been holding him down since the day he went away and was keeping it tight just for him.

As soon as they sat down they were ready to order. Crystal had grabbed a menu while they were waiting. Jada ordered their appetizers. She had chosen spinach artichoke dip and the mozzarella cheese sticks. After placing the order for the appetizers Jada ordered her main course. She ordered the Bourbon Street Chicken and Shrimp, Crystal had the Fiesta Lime Chicken, and Kierra had the Chicken Tenders platter.

"That sure was good. I know I had to be hungry. I don't even like Applebee's." Kierra said as she rubbed her full belly.

"I know." Crystal agreed.

"Well, ladies." Jada stood up as though she was about to leave.

"Where the fuck you think you going?" Crystal asked Jada.

"I am going to the Broadway." Jada turned to walk away and headed to the door.

Kierra looked at Crystal and followed Jada out the door. Crystal sat and watched her friends as they left without paying for their food. She looked around the room. She watched as all the patrons giggled and made small talk. She realized no one was looking in her direction. She didn't see not one Applebee's worker in site. The waitress hadn't even bought out the check. She decided to go ahead and make her escape before the waitress returned.

The three of them walked into the nightclub as though they didn't just run out on their check. Kierra led them through the club. She was looking for a table or a nice section to occupy. Jada was holding down the back. She tapped Crystal on the arm as she stopped to talk to her new friend.

"I think you are following me," Jada said to Bryson as she screamed in his ear. She was making sure he could hear her over the loud music.

Bryson smiled with a devilish grin, "This my little hangout. I am here all the time."

Jada looked Bryson over. His dreadlocks were freshly twisted. They were neatly braided towards the back. He had a fresh lining.

Bryson was wearing a crisp white tee with Rock Revival written in red across his chest and light blue stonewashed Rock Revival jeans. She tried to check out his belt, but his shirt was covering it. She could tell it was expensive because she could smell the fresh leather. When she looked down and noticed he was wearing some exclusive retro black, red and white air Jordan's, she figured that he had a few coins.

The waitress walked over to Bryson and handed him his drink.

"What are you drinking?" Bryson asked Jada.

"Whatever you drinking." Jada smiled.

Bryson pulled out his cellphone and sent a text message. The same waitress who had just walked away returned with Jada's drink.

Crystal looked back and realized that must have been Jada that had tapped her. She grabbed Kierra's arm. As she turned around, Crystal pointed in Jada's direction. It was no sense of her trying to talk over the loud music. They stood and waited on Jada for a minute. When they noticed Jada wouldn't be coming anytime soon, they both walked off and found them some seats.

Jada wiggled, giggled and sipped on the Hennessy and Coke as the club's DJ played Lil Wayne and 2 Chainz's "Rich as Fuck". She leaned in towards Bryson, "You know you are a taller and cuter version of 2 Chainz!"

Bryson gave Jada a side-eye looked and smile, "That's my cat but I hear that a lot." Bryson took a sip of his drink.

Chapter Six

Kierra, Jada, and Crystal left out the club together. They stood to wait as Jada said her see you laters and I will call you as soon as I charge my phone spill. Crystal and Kierra had decided to join Bryson after they noticed Jada was on her fourth drink. They knew that Jada probably would have left with this stranger had they not intervene. She was good at disappearing with folks when she found her something hot.

They talked briefly and Jada let them know her phone had died so she was going straight home. She figured that Brittany had possibly tried to call her but her phone had died an hour ago. They waited as all parties were in their cars. They pulled off the parking lot and headed in their respected destinations.

Kierra told Crystal to drop her off at Dom's house. Dominique had gone to elementary school with them. They met him during the fifth grade when Brittany's tragedy struck. He was a new transfer from St. Paul, Minnesota. He and Kierra were on and off again. Dominique was in an R & B singing group called the Carter Boys. The Carter Boys consisted of Dominque's two brothers, Donald and David, and their cousin Steve. Donald played the drums and David played the bass guitar. Steve was the pianist, well the keyboarder, he didn't transport his piano around. He only carried his keyboard. The Carter Boys fan base was huge in St. Louis. They opened up at major concerts only in St. Louis. The played a regular venue on Thursday nights at a club called the Signature Room.

Dominque had the smooth sound and swag of R. Kelly but he looked like Bruno Mars. Once he started getting the attention from all the girls Kierra was a consistent fixture in his life. They were more on than off if she had anything to do with it.

Crystal pulled up in front of Dom's house. Kierra opened the door and bent down to look at Crystal.

"How do I look?" Kierra asked Crystal.

Crystal looked and smiled as she admired her cousin's smooth beautiful mahogany skin tone and sexy perched lips. Crystal could see that Georgia's peach derriere protruding from the side. She and Brittany still had those washboard abs they had during their track days.

"I would say you looking like Gabrielle Union but I would be lying." Crystal chuckled, "Girl, shut my door. Dom standing at the door waiting on you."

Kierra looked back over her shoulder and seen her man standing on the porch with his shirt off. "Let me let you go. Text me when you get home so I know you made it." Kierra shut the door and walked towards Dom's house.

Dom and Steve shared an apartment on the city's Northside. Steve was never there, so Dom pretty much had the place to himself. They kept a nice clean bachelor pad. It was nicely furnished with updated appliances and every piece of technology and music equipment throughout the house.

As soon as they got inside the house Kierra gave him a tight embrace and Dom returned it with a sloppy kiss. Kierra moved her hands to unbuckle his pants.

"Slow your roll, ma. We got work to do." Dom took a step back and pointed to the Apple notebook on the glass table.

Kierra turned and look at the laptop. Dom had already had the Coldwell Banker Gundaker School of Real Estate website pulled up. His debit card was on the keyboard of the Apple product.

Kierra shook her head, "Dom, I was going to register and pay that three hundred eighty-five dollar at the beginning of the year."

Dom looked at Kierra, "I know what you said, but they have evening classes are starting January 13th. It's a weeklong class. You can be finished with the class which should prepare you to pass the test, and by the summer be selling houses. You need to get this done now! You are not getting none of this until that app is completed." Dom patted his package.

Kierra thought about her plans of selling houses and being able to purchase one of those abandon schools and make it to the living facility for teen moms. Her plan was to turn classrooms into bedrooms, use the cafeteria as the place where parents cooked learning how to make healthy meals. She planned on using the gymnasium to host plays, book events for local authors, parties and have a permanent venue for the Carter Boys.

Kierra sat down and completed the application. Once she entered Dom's credit card information and press submit Dom kept his promise. He led Kierra to his bedroom. He lit a few candles that he had sporadically placed around his bedroom, blue-toothed his phone to the speaker and let John Coltrane due to the rest. Kierra chuckled and grabbed his phone to turn his blue-tooth off. She pulled out her phone and hooked it up to the free standing speaker. She let him know the type of mood she was in when Adina Howard's *Freak Like Me* followed by Silk's *Freak Me*. An R. Kelly mixed tape ended their night.

Kierra had drifted off to never, never land after her sex workout with Dom. She laid in her wetness too tired to move. She grabbed her phone realizing that Crystal hadn't called or texted her. She reached over Dom who was sound asleep and retrieved her cell phone.

Just as she thought not a missed call or text. She dialed Crystal and she didn't answer. Then she dialed Jada and it went straight to voicemail. She was about to wake Dom up so he could take her home or at least make sure everyone's car was where they were supposed to be. Then she called Brittany.

With a craggy tone in her voice, Brittany said, "Hello."

"I am sorry to wake you but I am trying to see if Jada is there and if Crystal made it home."

Brittany was staying in the spare bedroom at Jada's place. She walked to the bathroom, "Crystal called me some time ago. She was about to go to bed. You know she had to tell me about the night that I missed."

"She could have done that at work in the morning," Kierra said.

"Well, she had some shit to say she didn't want everybody to hear." Brittany chuckled with scragginess. Brittany had laid her phone down on the edge of the sink, washed her hands and then dried them while keeping her phone up to ear with a hunched shoulder.

Kierra rolled her eyes, "Well, I am glad to know everyone is safe and sound. So, I will see you girls in the next few hours at work."

Brittany walked to Jada's room to ask her had she talked to Crystal. To her surprise the bed was empty, "This damn girl done went on a secret rendezvous and didn't say shit to me," Brittany said as she looked at Jada's empty unmade bed.

Chapter Seven

Crystal stood at the kitchen counter crushing up her mom's Tylenol with codeine. She poured four teaspoons of Dayquil in her blue thermal coffee mug. She used Dayquil instead of Nyquil so she wouldn't be nodding off at work. She added four shots of Vodka and topped it off with a Sprite. She swept the crushed pills off the counter with her hand into the mug. She stirred her concoction with a spoon and sucked the spoon dry before she put it in the sink. She was glad that Kierra was not there breathing down her back letting her know that wasn't a good choice.

Kierra only smoked her weed and drank on occasion. She had her limits. Addiction was not her friend and she wasn't about to dance with the devil like her parents chose to. Out of all the girls, Jada was the only one that got down on the Lean with Crystal.

Crystal knew she had to hurry up before her dad came to the kitchen for his morning cup of coffee. He had retired from his delivery duties and he had all his old friends that were now junkies working for him. He would get the merchandise from his supplier and either front them the work or let them pay to double for what he paid for it. Socks was the big hustle. He would sit at the table and bag up all kinds of socks. She didn't worry too much about her mom. She didn't wake up until noon.

Crystal pulled up to the Check 'N Go. She sipped on her dirty Sprite before she got out the car. She exited the car and observed her reflection through her car window. She was smiling from her euphoric feeling. Her chubby cheeks on her high cheekbones made her slanted eyes disappear she was smiling so hard. She was looking and feeling like a young Tasha Mack. Crystal pulled her Vince Cumato shades from her black fitted Peacoat pocket and placed them on her face. She dashed toward the building she spent eight hours of the day and five days a week. With a thermal coffee mug in hand, she entered her workplace.

Everyone knew what she was one when she entered with the shades on. Kierra couldn't even look in her direction. She looked over at Brittany, "You know we gonna have to watch her ass today."

Jada was telling them about her night when Crystal entered and hung up her coat. No one even acknowledges Crystal. They all were a bit disgusted. She didn't care she was in her zone. Everyone started telling Crystal that they needed their hair done and she just smiles and nodded to her own beat. She was so far gone she didn't even notice Brittany put the closed sign up in her window.

"Jada, we are gonna have to meet this Mandingo. Well, I mean Bryson." Kierra chuckled.

Jada looked at Brittany and pointed, "B, know how fine he is. She was with me when I met him at the laundromat."

Brittany couldn't finish counting the money of her customer fast enough. Hate grew in heart for an individual she never personally met. Her skin became flush and she appeared as though something had startled her. Then she remembered that Danitra had never called her back. She called Danitra only to receive some bad news. Mrs. Harris had died. She had fallen down her steps and broke her neck.

Brittany was at a loss for words. Her grandmother's friend had gone on to glory. Her emotions were all over the place. Before Danitra could go on with her story, Brittany remembered her last conversation with Mrs. Harris.

Mrs. Harris was exiting the Metro Call-A-Ride which provided curb-to-curb van service in St. Louis City and County. Mrs. Harris had seen Brittany dropping Jarvis off at the daycare that morning. She wanted to know why he was still attending the daycare. As she exited the van looking like the mother of the church with her wig twisted. She called out to Brittany before she reached her front door.

"Brittany, honey let me talk to you for a second." Mrs. Harris waited on Brittany to move before she took another step.

Brittany turned around a chuckled to herself, as she seen Mrs. Harris feet bulging from some white two-inch heels. Brittany turned and met her on the sidewalk. Jarvis stood waiting on the porch. Although Mrs. Harris often smiled at Jarvis, her look was very intimidating so he keeps his distance and smiled with fear.

Brittany grabbed Mrs. Harris two grocery bags and Mrs. Harris led the way to her front door, "I see you and your birthday gift this morning. When I saw you, I was trying to figure out why he was still going to the day care. He should be in at least kindergarten by now. You know he supposed to be in school right."

Brittany chuckled as the crisp December chill gently rubbed across her face. She thought to herself even in the dead winter Mrs. Harris had no off days. She waited as Mrs. Harris unlocked the door, Mrs. Harris looked back at her, and "If my memory serves me correct you had him after you graduated on your birthday?" Mrs. Harris opened the door and Brittany moved passed her to place the two bags in her kitchen.

"Yes, Mrs. Harris, I had him on my birthday the year I graduated high school. He still goes to the day care because the day care van does drop off and pick up at his school. My work hours don't allow me enough time to get him to and from school."

Brittany paused as she saw Mrs. Harris's bedroom set where her dining room once was. Mrs. Harris saw that it caught her attention as she walked down her hallway to meet back up with her at the front door.

"Yeah, I see you noticed my bed. My son moved it for me the last time he was here. This old lady can't do those steps anymore. I haven't been up there in almost three years. The birds and squirrels could have gotten in and taken over. Hell, I could have people up there and don't know it."

Brittany laughed to herself as thought about how nosey Mrs. Harris was. If someone were in her house she would most definitely know about it. Brittany remembered the first time she went to Mrs. Harris's house. She went to give her grandmother the mail. The two of them were sitting in the kitchen gossiping and drinking tea. Brittany was amazed that the house layout was just like theirs. Three rooms downstairs, the living room, dining room and the kitchen and four rooms upstairs; three bedrooms and the kitchen. The only difference between the two houses was that Mrs. Harris had her son turn the big walk-in closet on the first floor turned into a bathroom. She had only seen Mrs. Harris's son once. He was in the service and once he got out he stayed somewhere in California.

Although Mrs. Harris was her nosey neighbor they still looked out for each other. She was going to miss seeing those evil stares and that crooked black curly wig. Danitra went on tell her that Sean hadn't had any car problems lately. They had found his car in East St. Louis. It wasn't anything wrong with it this time. Danitra said, "That lil crazy bitch was playing hide and seek with Sean's car."

Brittany wanted to ask her had she seen Leslie on the news but she decided against it. Then she wanted to know about the scratches that were on the car but she decided against that too. In the beginning, she only knew her as Sean's side chic but when her picture was all over the news, she learned the side chic's actual name. Leslie was edged in her thoughts along with the terrified look she had as blood was seeping from her forehead.

She wanted Danitra to bring up Leslie to her. She knew Danitra had to have seen it on TV. The news came on right after her favorite daytime soap, The Young and the Restless. When Danitra didn't mention Leslie, Brittany had a feeling brewing inside that it had to be a reason. Danitra was usually a very talkative person. She would talk about the latest shopping deals she came across and any gossip she had heard. Today was different and Brittany realized it. There was some sort of disconnect. The dry conversation taking place between the two of them, indirectly let Brittany know that Danitra was involved with the disappearance of Leslie. Brittany just didn't know how she was involved. She evaded asking Danitra any questions, she was not trying to end up like Mrs. Harris or Leslie Collins.

Jada and Kierra sat watching Brittany's every move. They were impatiently waiting to hear what happened. Jada and Kierra sat trying to read Brittany's face expression. Brittany usually tried to manage her face expressions when she notices it may have shown what she was thinking. At that moment she didn't care about what her face may have shown or what they could be interpreted. She was amongst family and she knew they would bring her comfort.

Jada saw the same face that Brittany displayed when Mrs. Neal, their elementary teacher, nodded her head signaling Brittany to respond to the intercom call instructing her to go to the principal's office. Brittany's adult face displayed hurt and confusion. They couldn't wait until Brittany ended the call. Jada and Kierra could tell Brittany was at a loss for words. Her face told it all. Danitra placed Brittany on hold to retrieve another call. When she got back on the phone she let Brittany know she had to call her back. She had a family emergency. Her cousin who had only been in town a month had been arrested on some trumped up drug charges.

Brittany had sat there holding the phone long after Danitra had hung up. She needed someone to talk to but she didn't know who could keep her secret. She wanted to call her brother. She decided against it. She thought he may confide in his future baby momma and then she figured she would tell her friend or friends. Brittany stopped worrying about it. She just needed to keep her friend away from the person that killed the missing girl whose picture was plastered across the city. The same person Danitra failed to mention and Brittany was not trying to find out why.

Over two weeks ago, she had seen a murder take place right outside her bedroom window. There were posters spread throughout the city which pictured Leslie Collins face with missing stamped on it. The news was still reporting her being missing during their broadcast. It was at least three people who knew that Leslie would never return and her friend Jada had just spent the night with one of those people.

Their work evening was coming to an end and Crystal had sobered up and was able to partake in the plans they were making for the New Year. They were going to bring the New Year in with just the four of them. They had planned to have a vision board party and Crystal and Jada were in charge of gathering the magazines.

As they were about to walk out the door Jada's cell phone rang. Jada usually didn't answer numbers that were not saved to her contacts. This was an unfamiliar number and the time it came through was strange. No one typically called her around this time. Her mother would call her every now and them. She usually had the same number for a few months. Jada answered thinking her mother may have been in need of some money because that was the only time she would hear from her. She had a weird expression written all over her face while she held the phone to her ear. When she ended her call she let them know that some women had just called her to let her know that Bryson had been arrested and he would call her as soon as he was able to. Jada wanted to question the call. She wanted to know why she was contacted. Jada didn't consider herself his girlfriend. They hadn't really spoken about that. Jada and Bryson's bodies only had the dialogue. She had just not too long ago met Bryson. Jada didn't feel that she was important enough to receive that type of call. She nonchalantly responded okay before she ended the call.

Teresa Seals

Chapter Eight

You have a collect call from, Jarvis. An inmate in Southeast Correctional facility. This call is subject to be recorded. To accept the charges, dial eight. To deny the charges dial nine.

Brittany listened to the recording and started not to answer. She didn't know why he always called to get confirmation she was coming to the visit. Every time she told him she was coming, she made it. Brittany knew he didn't want to be disappointed. Jarvis would mention every now and again on how he didn't expect her to be there holding him down. He thought the once known high school track star would eventually run from him taking his son with her. She pressed eight and waited for the call to be connected, "Hello, Jarvis."

"Hey, B, Happy New Year's Eve! I was calling to see if you are still coming?"

"I am in the parking lot right now. I just parked when the phone began to ring. I started not to answer but I didn't want you to panic." Brittany didn't laugh.

"You didn't bring my son. I don't want him to see me caged like an animal." This was how the typical are you here conversation would go. He knew she was not bringing their son. They had agreed that wouldn't happen. Together they decided that when Jarvis, Jr. was old enough that they wouldn't even mention his whereabouts and would somehow try to avoid it when their son was old enough to ask.

Brittany felt that her son had an idea. He was not the average four-year-old. She figured that he realized that his parents were avoiding telling him his dad whereabouts.

"News flash buddy, animals receive better treatment than humans. Do you recall Mike Vick? Muhammad Ali made a living beating people over the head as commentators and spectators watched. But, you put dogs up to do a similar act, and all kind of animal rights people will be gunning for your ass. Anyway, he is with Jada. They're getting last minute stuff for our vision board party. We are bringing the New Year in at Jada's place and we are going to do this vision board thing-a-ma-jig."

"What's the purpose of that?" Jarvis asked.

Brittany didn't understand why he was keeping her on the phone. They could have discussed the vision board topic during her six-hour visit. Since he insisted keeping her on the phone, she continued, "Well, the purpose is to put everything you want out of life on the board. You think about your goals in areas such as finances, careers, personal growth and relationships. So, you place this board in an ideal area you will walk pass on a daily basis. It should inspire you and motivate you to achieve your goals. The board serves as a keepsake to keep you focused on your purpose in life."

Jarvis smiled. He had so much admiration for the mother of his child. The simplest things she said to him turned him on. He loved the fact that there were no limits for her. Nothing could stop her. Not even a mother that gave up on her. She was determined to succeed. He told her that he would see her once she got inside.

Brittany placed her phone in the armrest and grabbed her thirty dollars' worth of change along with her driver's license. She entered the facility. She was the fourth person in line. That was the incentive of getting there early. The wait time wasn't long. She walked pass two guards to walk up to the window where the guard was behind a glass similar to the one she sat behind at work to hand them her id. She informed the guard of the inmate's name and the guard gave her the inmates visiting to form to place her *John Hancock*. Brittany placed her signature on the form and walked to her left to line up behind the same individuals she was just behind when she first entered the facility. She was waiting her turn to enter the machine. This machine looked as though you were stepping in some sort of space shuttle. It was a little different from the body scan at the airport but it had its similarities. The sole purpose of this machine was to detect drugs and weapons.

Once she entered, she braced herself for the strong gust of air that would explore her enter body from all angles. The air wasn't hot, nor was it cold. The temperature was somewhere in between. After she left the machine she went behind one large door awaiting the next door to open so she could enter the visiting room. Inside the visiting room, she looked for a place to sit. She remembered the first time she came to visit Jarvis. The room was nothing she imagined. She thought once she entered the threshold the room would be dirty, gloomy, and dark. It was just the opposite. The room was bright with freshly painted white walls and a vending area to purchase drinks and snacks. During her first visit, she was so unprepared, they sat for six hours talking and drinking water from the fountain. Brittany was so hungry when she left, she blamed Jarvis for not informing her to bring money for the visit. He didn't know it was his first visit as well.

Brittany was so familiar with the process now. She had been coming for four years now. Brittany found the place she like to sit. She wanted a place where she realized she was free and would never allow herself to be caged. Brittany was not going to let anyone jeopardize that. Not even her closest friends. Brittany didn't run as much as she did in high school. She would occasionally go for a run but as she sat in the visiting room waiting on Jarvis, she saw herself running free. She chose a table near the window. The only view was the outdoor prison yard. She sat patiently waiting for Jarvis to enter the room. Brittany sat and watched as other inmates entered and visited with their visitors.

While waiting for Brittany drifted off in her thoughts thinking about Bryson and Leslie. Jada couldn't stop talking about this Mandingo warrior with the eight pack. Jada had her share of men but she never spoke about them they were she was currently talking about Bryson. The image that Brittany saw was completely different. Brittany saw a man with no conscious. She saw someone who would terrorize the world with evil. Brittany feared Bryson. She was a witness to what he was capable of doing. She was so deep in thought that she didn't see Jarvis as he approached her. Jarvis reached out to embrace her and she should stood up to greet him. He returned the embrace with a quick peck on her lips and they both took their seats.

Jarvis smiled showing his pearly whites, "What were you thinking about? Your little vision party or something?"

"No, smart ass I was actually thinking about a murder," Brittany said with her matter of the fact tone.

"Damn, you plan on killing me and I am not even a free man. That's harsh. Where's the love?" Jarvis joked.

Brittany smiled at his sarcasm, "No, silly." Brittany went on tell him about a situation she had no made her dilemma, "One night I was sleep and this noise woke me up. I looked at the side and saw Sean's girlfriend keying his car."

Jarvis interceded, "Sean's girlfriend? Isn't he and Danitra still married?" His eyebrows arched as if he were Ice Cube with a look of confusion.

"Yes, Jarvis, Sean, and Danitra are still married. Let me finish please." Brittany took a deep breath and leaned into whisper so no one could hear here, "So, as she was keying his car, I went to grab my cell phone. As I was getting my phone, I could hear people talking. It was like they were mumbling about a dispute. It kind of seem as though they were being discreet," Brittany closed her eyes, opened them quickly, and took another deep breath, "I make it back to the window

59

and it's the 2 Chainz looking dude towering over her body. They exchanged a few words and then he shot her. He shot her at point blank range. He didn't fret. He actually looked like he got some sort of thrill. He did it with such ease. That shit was scary. I watched her body just dropped to the ground. Her eyes were still open and then Sean's car was gone that morning. A few weeks later I call Danitra and she tells me Sean's got his car back and Mrs. Harris is dead."

Jarvis was giving her the side eye, "Do you think this dude is behind setting your crib on fire?"

Brittany shook her head. When the fire inspector gave his report it was due to the towel she left on the stove. He was a friend of her mother so he said the causes were unknown so that she wouldn't have any problems with the insurance. Brittany continued talking to Sean, "One day, Jada and I are at the laundromat and 2 Chainz walks in."

"The real 2 Chainz?" Jarvis was trying to be comical at the wrong time. Brittany looked at him as though she was calling him everything but Jarvis. Jarvis smiled to let her know he felt what her face had just displayed at that moment, "Did he recognize you?"

"No, he never saw me. When he put her in the trunk of Sean's car he looked around and I ducked down so he couldn't see me. That's not the worse part." She paused and looked him directly in his eyes, "Jada is fucking the dude."

"Was she messing with him before this happened or after?" Jarvis asked as if he were a detective.

"Her ass hooked up with him while we were at the laundromat, but he locked up for now. The caller let her know that it was about some bogus as drug charges."

"So you think he killed Mrs. Harris?"

"Hell yeah! That lady stopped going upstairs and they claim she fell down the stairs and broke her neck. His ass broke her neck. He must have seen Mrs. Harris watching him. Come to think about it, she wasn't outside the next morning when I was talking to Danitra. She wasn't even outside when my house was on fire." Brittany sat back in her chair and began to think.

"I don't understand why you haven't told Jada. What if he does something to her?"

"You know I can't tell Jada about the murder. She was like an old refrigerator that can't keep anything. I just have to figure out how to keep her away from him."

"Well right now he in jail and his only way of contacting her is the phone. So get rid of her phone. That way she will have to get a new one." Jarvis thought that would solve Brittany's issue.

"Jarvis, she will get a new phone and have the same number. He still will be able to call her." Then Brittany paused. It was as though the light bulb lit up over her head, "I am going to have to convince her to switch carriers. That way she will have a new number."

Jarvis went on tell her Brittany she could thank him later. He thought he had really brought the issue to an end and Jada wouldn't be in this guy's reach. Brittany didn't know that he knew where Jada lived. He may not have remembered the address to write but he knew how to get there. Jarvis and Brittany got up from the table and took a walk around the visiting room and made their way to the vending machine. They purchased a few snacks and some drinks, then headed back to their seats.

Jarvis sat and admired Brittany's beauty. He was longing to touch her soft caramel skin. He thought about his son and how he needed to be able to provide for his family once he was released. He had only four years left on his sentence. He looked at Jada, "I hope I am a part of your vision board?"

Jada smiled. She had only been with him and had turned down in potential man that approached her. "Of course you are a part of my vision. You have to ask."

"Yes, I have to ask. I am here rehabilitating myself. I read so I want to lose focus. This place will break you if you are weak. To be confined, removed from family and live in a cell will mess up your mind. I escape every day. I am in the library reading and in my cell reading. I just don't know what to expect on the outside of these doors. I will be labeled a felon the rest of my life. While I am here I supposed to be paying my debt off. When I walk out this door it's as though I am not a citizen. I have lost my voting privileges. What place will hire me so I can make a decent income to provide for my family?" Jarvis shook his head and had to regain his self-control. He was on the verge of breaking right there in front of Brittany.

Brittany reached out and grabbed his hands. She looked him directly in his eyes, "We will get through this. You will be your own boss. You have to find something meaningful to you. Jarvis, you have a purpose. You have the potential to be anything you put your mind to. Jarvis, you need to take that the world is mine approach. Baby, there are no limits to what you can do! Bring forth what is in you and run with that. These walls can't hold you forever. Everything will be okay. You just need to believe that it will." Brittany thought about how well her brother was doing and figured that Jarvis could take a similar path.

Jarvis looked at the clock and notice they had only thirty minutes left together, "Aye why don't you take my son over there with my moms and pops. He doesn't need to be with all you girls tonight."

Brittany agreed and Jarvis let her know he would give Janice a call. He had already talked to his mother early during the week. She had mentioned to him; it had been a minute since she seen her grandson. Janice wanted to see him and get to know him. She and her husband wanted to be a part of their grandson's life. Janice knew she would have to reach out to Brittany because she would never call her and ask her to watch her son. Janice didn't want to hear the word no. Janice didn't know if Brittany was upset with her son. Janice somehow figured that since Jarvis was locked up that Brittany wanted to keep any reminders of his existence away from her child. That was not how Brittany felt. Janice only felt that way because that would have been the attitude she had.

The two-hour drive to Jarvis skated by. Brittany pulled on the parking lot and seen Crystal's car. She figured that she and Kierra had come together. The two of them didn't believe in driving their own car to the same place they would just alternate who would be driving. As Brittany was getting out of her car, her cell phone rang. She had to sit back down to retrieve her phone from the armrest. She smiled when she noticed it was Jarvis's mom. His mom let her know she was willing to keep him and she would pick him up. Brittany let her know how to get to Jada's apartment. She let her know she would be there in an hour to pick her grandson up.

Brittany entered Jada' apartment. She was glad that she stayed on the first floor because at that moment she didn't want to climb any steps. Brittany chuckled about the steps as she thought about she had not been running lately. She remembered the only time she took a break from running was when she was pregnant with her son. She had been offered a scholarship to Jackson State University due to her running skills. Jarvis, Jr. was the result of her not attending the university.

Brittany reached the apartment door and she could hear the laughter as she entered the apartment building. She opened the door and became startled when she noticed a dread head individual sitting on the floor playing with her son. She looked around the apartment. She could see Jada preparing the food and Crystal were assisting her. Then she looked back and finally noticed Kierra standing in front of the TV thumbing through the channels. She became filled with anger as she seen her friends carrying on as though her son wasn't sitting on the floor with a stranger in the place she was currently calling home. She took a step in the apartment and slammed the door. Everyone jumped even her from how hard she slammed the door. Brittany's face was filled with frustration.

"Damn you here! So what!" Jada said as she walked out of the kitchen area, "Don't be coming here with all that noise because you are sexually frustrated."

Crystal following behind Jada, "I take it you didn't have a very good visit?"

Then the dread head stood up and went to reach for Brittany. She moved back out of his way.

"Damn, B, what's up?" Brandon asked.

"Boy, when did you get this mess in your head?" Brittany asked as she pushed her brother in his head.

"I bought them. These are dread extensions. I didn't want to grow through that growing process. So I cheated." Brandon said as he followed Brittany in the kitchen.

"I don't like them. You should get rid of them. You fitting a profile." Brittany said with an attitude. His dreads weren't as long as Bryson's dread. She felt kind of stupid for even thinking that Bryson was even in the apartment in the first place.

"B, I am already fitting a profile. My hair isn't going to change nothing." Brandon was waiting on Brittany to pull the momma card. She had been telling him what to do since they were small children.

"How's your girlfriend and when is the baby due?" Brittany looked at her little brother as she bit into the stuffed mushrooms Jada had made. She walked into the bedroom she was using while she was staying with Jada. Brandon followed her.

"Demeasha is fine and we are expecting February 14th." Brandon followed Brittany and grabbed his own stuffed mushroom.

"What brings you to my neck of the woods?" Brittany asked.

"Well, I stopped by to see you and my nephew. I was going to see if you would let him hang out with me."

"You know I don't mind but his grandmother is on his way to get him."

"Pat in town?" Brandon asked with confusion wondering why no one had told him his mother was visiting.

"No, little brother. He is going with Jarvis's mom, Janice. She is on her way to pick him up." Brittany went to pack his overnight bag he hadn't use since he spent the night with her aunt Alexis.

"Does he know he's going with his grandmother?" Brandon asked.

She looked at her brother, "Damn! I didn't tell him because it just came up today." She stuck her head out the bedroom door, "Jarvis, come here baby."

Brittany went on to tell Jarvis that he was going with his grandma Janice. She thought he was going to be upset but he wasn't. He saw her briefly on Christmas when she and his grandpa dropped off all the clothes and cool gifts. Although he didn't spend a lot of time with his grandparents he loved when he did. They treated him like a little king.

Brandon and Jarvis had gone. The girls had completed their vision boards and drank the four bottles Freaky Moscato wine all up. Kierra vision board had a real estate theme. Jada vision board was labeled *Pink Legacy Boutique* with clothes, jewelry and shoes precisely placed on her board. Crystal's board had money, different exotic cars and places she wanted to travel to. Brittany used words such as editor, journalist, international blogger, a picture of Oprah and written herself a million-dollar check.

The night ended with good conversation and plans for the New Year. Everyone went to check Crystal's wine glass once she started talking about robbing their workplace. They were smelling it thinking she had more than just wine. Kierra wanted to make sure it wasn't the dirty Sprite doing the crazy talk.

Chapter Nine

Jada walked into Brittany's bedroom. She was moving stuff around. Then she called out to Brittany, "Brittany, let me see your phone!" She didn't care that Brittany was in a deep sleep. She was on a mission to find her phone. Anxiety began to kick in and she was having small panic attacks. People cherished a lot of material items that held some sort of sentimental value. Her phone happened to be near and dear to her heart. She thought about all the pictures that were stored on her phone. Jada considered her phone her lifeline. Her lifeline was being interrupted. She was acting as is if she were being attacked by asthma. Jada was really being dramatic. It was as though her chest was tightening, she was experiencing shortness of breath, and reoccurring periods of wheezing.

Brittany reached under the cover with her eyes still closed and handed her phone to Jada. Jada stood over Brittany, "I need you to unlock it." Brittany unlocked her phone and handed it back to Jada. She could hear the sadness in how Jada was speaking. She opened her eyes. Brittany looked at Jada and became frightened. She had never seen Jada act in such away. Jada never performed in that manner when her mother made a bunch of broken promises. Jada was showing transparency on how she felt with the loss of her phone.

Jada dialed her own number and walked around the house listening for it to the ring. Then she called Kierra and asked her did she pick up her phone by mistake. She hung up from Kierra and called

Crystal to ask her about her phone. Jada had reached her boiling point. She sat down on the couch and was trying to remember what she had done. Then she remembered she and Crystal had stepped outside to smoke a blunt. She walked outside a looked around near the bush they were standing by. She paced back and forth. Then she went behind the bush knowing the phone wouldn't be back there. When she came back in Brittany was standing there waiting for her.

"You haven't found it yet," Brittany asked a redundant question. She knew the only way she would have found her phone if she had gone and looked in the apartment's complex trash can. When she and Crystal stepped outside, Brittany grabbed the phone, turned it off and put it in the trash she took out while they were standing outside smoking.

If looks could kill Jada would have shot Brittany down where she stood. Brittany was usually the one who displayed the expressions with her face. The roles were now reversed. Brittany could feel the animosity and Jada's face told her to not say another word. Brittany remained quiet. She just watched Jada as she moved back and forward. Jada looked in the refrigerator, opened every cabinet door in the kitchen, and took the empty bag out of the trashcan. Brittany thought she was going to want to look in the trash when she noticed the bag was empty.

Brittany didn't really feel apprehensiveness about what she had done but she knew she needed to stroke Jada's ego, "That may be the sign you needed to go get you a new phone. Wasn't your screen cracked?" Brittany didn't give her a chance to reply. She continued, "I will ride with you to go get another phone. T-Mobile is running a special. They have unlimited data and some more stuff. I believe it's cheaper than what you were paying being with Sprint." Brittany was praying she would agree. She didn't want to keep talking and appear to be guilty.

"I guess I could get a new phone. I have been thinking about that pickup and go stuff. I am tired of being in contracts. Damn, but my pictures though." Jada couldn't get passed the fact that she had some memorable moments on her phone.

"All your pictures are backed up to your Gmail account." Brittany had all the answers. This whole situation was suffocating her thoughts and feelings. She had no one she could really talk to about the whole ordeal. Brittany considered herself as doing the right thing in trying to protect her friend from the unforeseen misfortunes they could occur when it came to Jada dealing with Bryson. She was praying for a miracle. Brittany was deeply concerned with the safety of her friend but she just couldn't find the right words to convey the message. She didn't know how the relationship of Jada and Bryson would play out. Brittany didn't want to phantom the idea of Jada falling in love with this murderer. Brittany was going to continue to be in the mix until Bryson was out of the picture.

She dropped the heavy load of uneasiness she was carrying when Jada agreed to her new phone idea. They both went to get ready and was heading to Jada's new cell phone place.

The girls sat in silence as they were on their way to T-Mobile. Brittany's head was hung low. Jada looked her over a few times.

"Girl, what's wrong with you?" Jada said out of concern.

Brittany pulled herself together. She hated that her face told her thoughts. She lied, "I am just thinking about my grandmother's house and what my mom is going to do. Kierra told me she was about to start real estate school and she had met some old guy who was going to mentor her. She said she will help me find a place but I don't think my income will suffice."

"B, Crystal and I have been telling you what we need to do!" Jada smiled. Jada and Crystal came up with the idea of just to take the money from the Check 'N Go and just run. There was no clear plan of how they could get away with stealing from their place of employment.

"Those braids are too damn tight on your head Queen Latifah wanna be. You old Jada Pinkett-Smith reject. I am not about to set it off with you and your home girls. You can quit pressing me about that. Y'all better come up with a plan B." Brittany said in her matter of the fact tone.

"Damn!" Jada yelled causing Brittany's body to jolt as she slammed on the breaks.

Brittany slowly turned her head to position her eyes in Jada's direction, "What the problem?"

"I just thought about Bryson not being able to call me." Jada never took her eyes off the road.

Hearing the name Bryson was just dreadful to Brittany's ears. She didn't even know how to respond. Just as she was about to speak, Jada caught her off, "Well, I really don't have to worry about him calling. He knows where I stay so if he's really interested when he gets out he may just pop up at my door. I know," Jada began to sing her version of En Vogue's *Giving Him Something He Can Feel*, "I gave him something he could feel to let him know that I am real!" Jada turned on to T-Mobil's parking lot.

Brittany searched for the words as she tried to read Jada's body language. She couldn't be that serious Brittany thought. Brittany wanted to tell her that she barely even knew him. She wanted to know what made him different from Andre. Andre's name was off limits. Brittany wanted to bring him up but she couldn't. When he was out the picture Jada, Brittany, Crystal, and Kierra vowed to never bring his name up.

Jada met Andre the night of their graduation. She and Andre had dated for three years. Andre was tall, dark, and handsome. He liked

70

to box. He had established Beats by Dre long before Dr. Dre of N.WA. Jada had to find out the hard way. Brittany looked towards Jada's direction and didn't want to seem too excited, "Well, if he liked the way you all carried on, he'll be back." Brittany was referring back to Jada's she gave him something he could feel statement. Brittany realized that Jada mentioned that Bryson knew where she stayed, "He knows where you stay?"

Jada opened the door to exit the car, "Yep!"

Brittany watched as Jada pranced her way into T-Mobile. Getting rid of the phone was not enough. Jada had been in several relationships and Brittany didn't even understand why Bryson would be that one person she was even worried about calling. She collected herself along with her thoughts and headed into T-Mobile to join her friend.

Brittany cell phone rang. She looked down and seen it was Kierra, "Hello." Brittany said dryly.

"Dang, Debbie Downer. Did I catch you at a bad time?" Kierra could hear and feel disappointment coming through the phone." Kierra thought that Brittany was caught up in her emotions about her current living arrangements. Brittany was using that as an excuse to her being concerned about Bryson and Jada. Being homeless should have been on the top of her list. Brittany knew she and her son had several places to go.

"I am good. I just have a lot on my mind. Did you find out about how soon we could be looking for me a place to stay?" Brittany waited on Kierra to respond.

"Not yet but I will when we hang up. I have two reasons for this call. First, I was calling to see if J found her phone. Second, I want to know if you girls want to go to New York or to the Mardi Gras next month." Kierra really didn't want Brittany to kill the excitement she had. It was hard for Kierra because Brittany's depression was seeping through the phone.

Brittany wanted to tell Kierra. Kierra was the most responsible one of the group. She held things together well. Even her parents' lifestyle didn't break her. She maintained very well. The only thing that stopped Brittany from sharing was Crystal and Kierra's relationship. The girls were close when it came to their circle but some information had a way of seeping out.

Dominque, Kierra's boyfriend, always looked at Andre like he wanted to make him disappear. Everyone knew that Kierra had to let him know what was going on. Crystal hung out at a barbershop on occasions to do hair. Brittany didn't want Dom or some patrons at the barbershop knowing what she witnessed.

Brittany was getting out the car while Kierra was talking. She entered the T-Mobile, "We are at T-Mobile now. I am here waiting on Jada to get done but I prefer going to New York. Let me ask Jada what she wants to do." Brittany walked over to Jada, "Kierra wants to know if you want to go to New York or the Mardi Gras next month?"

Jada was finishing up her transaction. She never looked in Brittany's direction as she answered, "NYC baby! I am trying to get at Fiddy! I am not flashing for no beads and I don't have time for no voodoo mess!"

"Voodoo!" Kierra laughed as she heard Jada's response, "New York it is. You all go ahead and get done. I am about to look up travel information and make reservations." Kierra ended the call before Brittany even responded.

Chapter Ten

Brittany, Jada, Kierra and Crystal were standing at the luggage carousel in LaGuardia Airport trying to retrieve their baggage. Crystal saw her purple polka-dot suitcase coming towards her. She reached in and snatched it up. Brittany spotted her bright lime-green suitcase and squeezed in between a couple to grab her luggage. She then pulled her phone out as she waited for Kierra and Jada's luggage to come around on the carousel.

"Kierra, what hotel are we staying?" Brittany asked.

"We are staying at the Hyatt in Manhattan. It supposed to be near Time Square." Kierra said as her eyes were glued to the carousel.

"We should have come here for the New Year, so we could have seen the ball drop," Crystal said.

No one even responded to Crystal. Jada and Kierra finally grabbed their luggage and the girls were headed towards the exit.

"I hope this cab ride is not very expensive. We are like thirty minutes away from Manhattan. I am not taking no train because I am not about to be lost so don't even mention it." Brittany looked over towards Kierra as she saw her looking at the information pertaining to the train. Brittany was glad they were on vacation. She could relax her nerves concerning with rather or not Bryson would just show up at their doorstep.

They checked into their hotel room, went up to their rooms to leave their luggage and was back outside. Kierra had e-tickets sent to her phone from the Big Bus Tours. As soon as they made it to the sidewalk a tour bus was pulling up.

This wasn't the best weather and they realized that as they were at the top of the tour bus. They went back down to the lower level. Their North Face jackets were not shielding them from the cool breeze.

Jada looked around and with excitement she yelled, "Awe look. We should have gotten on the TMZ tour bus. I betcha some type of star prolly over there! OMG! Fiddy might be on that baby. I have been looking for him ever since he said have a baby by me, be a millionaire." They all sniggered in unison at Jada as she seemed so serious about finding 50 Cent.

"We are the stars!" Kierra shot back.

When the tour bus made it to SoHo the girls made their exit. Everywhere they walked it was either an Asian man or woman holding a small portrait with pictures. In their dialect, you could make out them saying Coco Chanel, Louis Vuitton, Gucci, Coach and Michael Kors.

They decided to follow an Asian woman who had convinced them that she had the best deal on handbags. They entered a building. It was dark gloomy and dry. The walls in the building were faint. The white paint was dirty. The walls were so dirty that they were beyond beige. As they turned several corners of what appeared to be a maze to the elevator door. There was a man awaiting their arrival. The girls boarded the elevator. They made it to the floor and the doors open. They all laughed as the guy raised the steel aluminum door so they could exit. Three white women with three big black trashed bags entered the elevator as they were exiting.

The girls could hear the sounds of the sewing machines going wild. Signs were posted on gates stating and warning them not to take any photographs. They followed the arrows which directed them to a room. In this room were several handbags. They were wall to wall knock-off hands bags of every designer. The girls looked around and examined a few bags. They chose a few that could pass for the real deal. When everyone made their purchases they headed back to the elevator. They were lead right out a door which put them right on the sidewalk.

"Now why the hell we didn't come through that door instead of on going through a bunch of twists and turns!" Kierra laughed and they all joined her in laughter. The Asian lady had led them through a bunch of twist and turns. They had even ridden an elevator up to the floor where they made their purchases. In the end, they didn't do what they did while entering to exit. This fraud which was taking place was just as illegal as the drug trade. The individuals had to make sure they were not infiltrated for trafficking counterfeit goods.

They walked a few blocks not knowing where they were going until they noticed a tour bus. They showed their passes and boarded the bus. The tour bus passed by several attractions. Kierra, Jada, Brittany and Crystal admired the scenery as they listened to the commentary from the tour guide. The girl's chit chatted up until they made it back to where they originally boarded the tour bus.

Their second day in New York they were headed to Club 40/40. They stood in line about twenty minutes waiting to enter. Each girl had on all white attire. They passed by several jerseys in picture frames as they walked over to the area which contained a white sectional and sat down. They observed the men and women as they gathered and danced in their seats. They were all anticipating Jay-Z to make a guest appearance but it never happened. Jada was low key waiting on 50 Cent. She was watching every male counterpart that she saw.

Their time in New York came to an end. It wasn't exciting as they thought it would have been. Before they headed back to the airport the each got Jarvis a souvenir from the M&M's store.

Jada looked at her friends as they rode in the Taxi van headed to the airport, "We needed to have met some people from here so we could have actually toured the city. Not knowing where to go made this trip boring. I didn't even get to go to Harlem and see the Apollo. I am going to have to find me some New York friends on Facebook. So, when we come back we can get a real tour!"

The girls laughed in unison. They were in agreement with Jada but they felt that it was still a nice little getaway. This was all of their first trip outside of St. Louis. Kierra made a mental note to make better plans for their next trip. She knew with her phone in hand the world was at her fingertips. She could search the World Wide Web and find anything she wanted. Kierra was going to use that to her advantage during their next rendezvous.

Crystal's mom picked them up from the airport. When they made to Jada's apartment complex they couldn't believe their eyes. The brick building contained black burn stains, the windows were busted out and red danger tape went around the entire building. Jada was disappointed but Brittany couldn't believe her luck. She was trying to figure out why her life had turned into one big tragedy.

Chapter Eleven

As they entered *Crossroads Ministries of El Shaddai*, the choir was doing their rendition of VaShawn Mitchell's *Turn Around for Me*. Brittany, Jarvis, Jada, Kierra, and Crystal had made it in time to find a seat together on the pew five rows from the exit door. Brittany hadn't been to her grandmother's church since her funeral. She looked around and saw some familiar faces. There were a quite a few new faces. The guy that happened to be bringing Easter Sunday's sermon was very new to the congregation.

The Senior Pastor introduced Richard McCauley as the Assistant Associate Pastor. Richard McCauley appeared to have that Omari Hardwict swag but stood tall looking as though he was Tyler Perry. His bald head shined as he displayed his five o'clock shadow with a crisp lining. He spoke about he had had been resurrected from being the prodigal son. After he told the churchgoers about the power being in the name of Jesus and how he had been resurrected after he had spent ten years incarcerated in the federal penitentiary, he started literally stepping on the toes of the churchgoers. The applauses, Amens, and hallelujahs were spoken proudly. His last stop was the pew of Brittany, Jada, Kierra, and Crystal.

"You plan on being an army and rising up, but you rising up for all the wrong reasons and no purpose. There is no need to do that foolish thing. God will perfect you and those things are going to turn in your favor. You may be wounded in more ways than one. Today, I am here to tell you it won't work but the blood still works." He took a drink of water from the glass that was on the side of the podium and then continued, "Keeping secrets for unknown reasons. Those type of transgressions is small things to a giant. Lying, stealing, deceiving, and scheming is not conducive to your health nor for those around you. Making plans to prosper on paper but not taking the necessary steps to get there. Just yip-yapping. You have to put some work in if you really want to achieve the impossible. But, you are distracted. That loud has you where you can't hear or see. But, I guess that's only going to fall on deaf ears. Blog about your salvation, quit dressing up those lies, lift up that head as if that hair is slayed and know there is a lot of real-estate in the Kingdom. If you know HIM demons in hell can't turn you around. I am talking about the man who died on Calvary for you and me. HE's is better than Blue Shield, Blue Cross, and that Obama Care." The Associate Pastor ended by letting the churchgoers know he had never seen the righteous forsaken and then informed them that the doors of the church were open. At the time he may have been all over the place in his delivery but it was well received. Brittany wanted to tell Crystal that her idea of stealing for the job was not conducive to their health but she didn't. She didn't want anyone bringing up the keeping secrets part.

The church stood as the Senior Pastor, Associate Pastor, and the Deacons exited the sanctuary. They went to stand at the exit to greet the churchgoers as the exited the facility. Brittany had already informed the girls that she had to drop Jarvis off with his grandparents. They were having an Easter egg hunt at their church and they wanted him there with them.

Brittany entered the car after dropping Jarvis off with his grandparents, "We should have fellowshipped with them. It's all kind of food in there."

Jada pulled off the parking lot, "I don't eat everybody's cooking. You don't know if those folks washed their hands or keep a clean house."

Crystal looked over at Kierra as they sat in the back of Jada's new black Ford Expedition, "People kill me with that mess. They will walk in Ruth Chris, Pappadeaux, hell even Applebee's and folks order, then eat that cooking like they did it themselves."

Kierra and Brittany laughed in agreement. Jada knew she was right. She turned to Brittany to change the subject, "Who was that new pastor at your grandmother's church? I saw how he was checking you out."

Crystal chimed right in, "He did hug you longer than he did anyone else and he watched you as you walked away."

Kierra looked out the window as they pulled on the parking lot of Chili's, "Speaking of the devil!" She pointed to the direction of the Associate Pastor exiting his black Mercedes Benz.

Crystal and Jada chuckled as they all watched him along with three of the deacons they saw earlier at church entered the restaurant.

As Brittany was about to exit her cell phone rang. She looked down at her phone and seen it was Brandon. She told them she would catch up because she really needed to talk with him.

"Hello, little brother."

"Hey, B," Brandon said.

"I only saw my niece once and I'd been trying to get in touch with you. Jada and I just moved in this new place. We need you to come and do some work for us."

When they made it back from their New York trip, Jada's entire apartment building caught fire due to faulty wiring. Jada was relieved to find out that it was due to faulty wiring. Before they left for their trip Jada had found an old pack of Newport's. She smoked a few cigarettes with her bedroom window open and sprayed some Glade after each puff. She hadn't had a cigarette in so long that no one even realized that she had even stopped smoking. It was probably due to the fact that she occasionally fired up a blunt instead of the Newport. To most folks who are not addicted to cigarettes smoking is smoking and it didn't matter what type of smoking was taking place.

Brittany and Jada both moved in Brittany's aunt Alexis house until Kierra found them a house in their price range. Jada could have gone to her grandparents' house but she was afraid they would treat her like a little kid. Jada was not trying to have a curfew at her age. Kierra found them a house with two bedrooms, two baths, with a finished basement right outside the city limits. Kierra had her real estate license for two months. Brittany and Jada were her first sale. Kierra had hooked with this girl by the name of Robin Hughes. She was showing her all the tricks and the trades to real estate. Kierra was catching on fast. She put the money aside for the sale. Kierra was so proud of herself from the accomplishment. She was on to her next thing. Kierra had to find her location for her Diamonds in the Ruff program.

They were not far from their job, Check 'N Go. Jada and Brittany agreed to split the cost fifty-fifty. She had been trying to get in touch with Brittany's brother so they could do some remodeling. He agreed and they made a plan to start the next weekend. Brittany ended to call and entered the restaurant. She looked around for her friends.

She laughed to herself as she saw the men from the church sitting with her friends.

Brittany walked over to join them. Richard stood as she took her seat. He was seating across from the empty seat that had been waiting for her to arrive. "Now, what brought this about?" Brittany asked as her right hand pointed to the group in a circular motion as she took her seat inquiring about the seating arrangements. Richard took his seat after she sat down.

Brittany looked over at Jada and noticed that she was intrigued with whatever they were discussing near their end of the table. Brittany wanted to tell her that she needed to hold on to the little insurance money she did have because Brandon would be over to assist them with their remolding needs. She decided she would just wait. Then Brittany said a silent prayer. The guy Jada was talking to kind of favored 50 Cent. She was hoping he was saying all the right stuff. Britany prayed he would say something they would make Brittany forget all about Bryson. Everyone seemed as though the conversations they were having were therapeutic. She decided to talk to her seat partner since he was looking lonely being entertained with the other conversations taking place.

"So, Deacon, I didn't get your name." Brittany smiled.

"That's all you have? You didn't get my name, really?" he adjusted himself in his seat, "My name is Richard, but all my friends call me Richie. By the way, I am an associate pastor, not the deacon."

"Richie, you don't say?" Brittany chuckled. She wanted to ask him about his finances but she decided against it. She didn't want to come off as a gold digger. The entire time she sat engaged in conversation all she could do was think about Jarvis. Even though the meal and conversation were innocent, she just felt as though she was misplacing the loyalty amongst the father of her child. As the meal came to the end and Richie covered the cost for the entire party,

Brittany attitude changed. When he asked her for her number she obliged without any arguments.

Chapter Twelve

You have a collect call from, Jarvis. An inmate in Southeast Correctional facility. This call is subject to be recorded. To accept the charges, dial eight. To deny the charges dial nine.

Brittany waited before she'd press the number to accept the call. She placed herself in the proximity of her son. She didn't want to waste time getting him to come to the phone so he could speak to his father. He was in his room playing with his art easel. He looked up to his mother and kept on doing his little design he was creating.

"Hey, Jarvis," Brittany said as soon as she heard his voice. Jarvis, Jr. looked up and his face grew in excitement. He hated that his father was in the situation he was in but he loved hearing his father saying he loved him. Jarvis, Jr. never made mention to his mother that he knew his father was in jail. Since they failed to mention his whereabouts, he never asked. His young mind figured that his family was trying to protect his best interest. Jarvis would ask his son what he was reading. The child would sometimes grab a book and tell him the name. Then Jarvis, Sr. would follow with, "Son, you are a human being and always walk like a god. Never forget your hopes and dreams. Always remember people are calling for your demise. There is a right way to fight, so just do right! Dare to be different!"

Jarvis, Jr. could repeat that word for word. His father said that to him on every call. Jarvis, Sr. had written that to himself in an anger management class. He kept it his pocket and only read it when he was on the phone with his son. He wanted to teach him differently. He hoped and prayed that his son would be the best human he could be. At his young age, Jarvis, Jr. knew he made his own choices. He would let everyone he encountered know to dare to be different.

"Happy birthday, Brittany! What big plans do you and my son have for today?" Jarvis asked as the enthusiasm could be heard through the phone. He thought it was quite special that his son and girlfriend shared the same date of birth.

"We are going to have a little backyard slash housewarming get together right here in our new home." Brittany tried to make it as though it was no big deal. She never wanted him to feel as though he was missing out on much. She tried her best to protect his emotions when it came to family stuff. "Do you want to speak to your son?"

"Of course, I do!" Jarvis responded in a way that Brittany knew that was a real stupid question.

Brittany called out to her son and he ran over to her. She handed him her cell phone. Jarvis listened and nodded his head as if his dad could see him. Jarvis told his dad thank you. He finished with, "Dare to be different," and handed the phone back to his mother. Jarvis smiled with pride. He realized that his son was paying attention. That day and at that instant he realized that the moment he became free he knew he had to live his life in a way we would never no longer regret.

Brittany placed the phone towards her ear, "Your dad is coming to get him around five."

"Yea, my mom let me know that they get to see him a lot often now. How is this house thing working out with you and Jada?" Jarvis was really concerned about the fact that she made a life changing event with a friend and not him. He had no one to blame but himself but he needed to know where he stood when it came to his living arrangements once he was released. He didn't have a problem going to live with his parents but he wanted to be around his family.

"Well, Jada actually went in with me to make sure I was able to qualify for the home loan. She plans on moving downtown to a loft style or finding her a condo. I really can't wait until you see this place. It's somethings I want to do but I want to wait until you get here."

"Wait until I get there for what? You think I know how to do that type of work. The only thing I know how to do is cut hair. You better let Brandon take care of that."

"Brandon is taking forever. He came over and did some painting but I want him to knock this wall down so that you can see the dining room from the kitchen."

"Oh, you want an open floor plan?" Jarvis chuckled.

"Yes, that's exactly what I want. The living room is not that big. The dining area is huge and the way my HGTV system is set up, I vision a spacious entertainment area. Right now everything seemed so closed in." Brittany noticed the company with the table and chairs had arrived. She walked outside and showed them to the back. Jarvis told her he would call her back later. She thought that was quite strange because they only talked once on the day he called. She let him know she would be waiting on his call. Brittany really wanted to know what time he would be calling. She was trying to figure out and prepare herself when the call came through and Richie was around.

Brittany and Richie had been dating for the last month. Today was the first day that he would see where she resided. She always met him at the location. He never picked her up. Brittany had a crazy a way of thinking that somehow she was protecting Jarvis feelings for being so discreet.

Jada walked through the door with the birthday cake in her hands and noticed her disposition, "B, you good?"

Brittany looked at Jada as if she had just spoken a foreign language. She really didn't know how to respond.

"I get it. You working on the master plan on how we getting ready to set this major heist off."

Brittany walked up to Jada and placed her cell phone up to her head, "What's the fucking procedure when you have a gun up to yo head?"

"Frankie, you better get the fuck on!" Jada was quite agitated.

"Now you see how stupid you and Crystal sound every time y'all say something about setting it off. You better be making the best designs and getting the next person I feature on my blog to wear it during their photo shoot. That makes better sense than trying to rob our job."

Kierra and Crystal walked through the door as Jada walked away with the cake in her hand.

"B, I have a hot topic I know you would love the details about." Crystal waited on her to respond.

"You may as well have gone ahead a spill it before this house be filled with people or before you get high. You know when you on one you can't remember nothing." Brittany laughed.

"Well, I went to the barbershop early today and the hot topic was Richie Rich. Dudes were talking real heavy about him." Crystal was speaking as though she was Wendy Williams. She would pop in and out of her friend King's barbershop to do a couple of heads for extra money. His shop was located on the business intersection in St. Louis. You couldn't get through the city without going in the vicinity of St. Louis Avenue and Grand Avenue.

Everyone was tuned in waiting and holding on to every word that had just rolled off of Crystal's tongue. Before she continued she pulled out her blunt to light it.

"Um, you are going to have to put that out. Jarvis is in the other room." Brittany looked at Crystal with a stern look. She was more pissed about the gossip than the blunt. She waited for Crystal to put the blunt out before the conversation continued, "How do you know they were speaking about him?"

Crystal looked around for an ashtray and put her blunt on pause when she came across the ashtray. Crystal noticed Brittany looking at the faucet. Crystal ignored her. She was not about to wet her weed, "In the beginning, I was not quite sure if they were talking about him because they kept saying Richie Rich. Then someone made mention about seeing him at the church and he was doing charity events in the community. When they spoke on the Benz, I knew exactly who they were talking real heavy about then. Before he got jammed up he was real big out here in these streets." Jada, Kierra, and Brittany were tuned in as though Crystal was a news anchor on the five o'clock news. Crystal continued, "I don't want to perpetuate a whole bunch of negativity but how they put it, he may have a bounty on his head due to the fact he has been found in several people's paperwork. He allegedly has told on a few of his own family members. When he got jammed up he got a whole bunch of other people jammed up with him. He left the last chic he was fooling around without here scrambling. Richie Rich put this girl in some life or death situations. All I have to say is maybe he's a different person. You see he in church and all now."

Jada looked at her friends, "Yea, he may be a changed man due to the fact he all in church. If I were him, I would have started my life in a new place. Hell, I would have exhausted all cities before I came here. You know St. Louis is so big. Everybody know somebody. We can get on the Book and start lurking ain't no telling what we can find if it's not blocked. I wonder if his money still long."

Kierra started laughing, "Yes, somebody ugly ass daughter stays blocking me. I get all on Dominique's status. I am lurking and responding to people like they are talking to me. As soon as I comment, block." Kierra shifted her head and placed her hand on her chest as if she were clutching some pearls.

They all shared a laughed and headed outside to partake in the birthday festivities. Brittany had let Richard know that he could come when Jarvis had left with his grandparents.

Jarvis had left with his grandfather and the girls were laughing and chit chatting with the guest. Richard made his way to the backyard. The sun was working its way out. This June summer evening was experiencing some fall weather. St. Louis weather had been a quite bipolar and nothing new was taking place on this day.

Brittany noticed Richard and gave him a wave as she bought her conversation with her brother and his girlfriend, Demeasha, to an end. She was feeling him but this new found drama had her speculating on what her next move with him should actually be. Her only love interest had been Jarvis. Anyone else didn't stand a chance. Richard had begun to win her over. Her phone began to vibrate so she pulled it from her back pocket. When she noticed it was Jarvis, she headed inside to take the call.

You have a collect call from, Jarvis. An inmate in Southeast Correctional facility. This call is subject to be recorded. To accept the charges, dial eight. To deny the charges dial nine.

Brittany was anxious to know why she was receiving two phone calls in one day. The closest she became to two phone calls would only occur in a week, not on the same day. When the operator was done she pressed eight.

"Hello," Brittany tried not to show the tension she was experiencing.

"Hey, B, I know you are probably wondering why I am calling you back. Well, I wanted you to know I had my parole hearing three weeks ago. I didn't tell anyone about it because I didn't want anyone getting their hopes up high. I have three weeks left before I find out if it were approved or denied. I couldn't give you anything for your birthday but I thought I could share that with you."

Brittany paused. She didn't even know how to respond. She knew that time was approaching but she didn't expect it this fast. She thought she had to wait for him for at least four more years. Brittany was enjoying her time with Richard. She had never been wined and dined. Richard had made her a priority and they hadn't even been to second base.

Jarvis could hear that she was crying. He figured those were tears of joy. Brittany knew she had to decision to make and she didn't want to make it at that moment. She was enjoying on the way things were going with Richard. Jarvis let Brittany know he loved her and ended the call. Brittany wiped her tears and became startled when she saw Richard staring at her pain.

Richard stood in the shadows as he watched Brittany readjust her disposition. She turned around and was taken back. She didn't expect to see him standing there.

Richard looked around impressed with the décor. Although, the gray sectional was unique it didn't look expensive nor was it cheap. It just wasn't something his type of lifestyle would provide. He appreciated the fact that the set-up was plush. The light fixtures were extravagant. The silver accents accessories added to the detail.

"I see you have a little upscale taste. This décor looks like something out of a magazine." Richard walked towards Brittany as he stood in the hallway between the living room and the kitchen.

Brittany really wanted to be alone in her thoughts but she knew he had seen her crying. So, she was fighting portray that everything was okay.

"Yea, I should have waited on the furniture because I wanted to tear this wall down." Brittany touched the wall that sectioned off the kitchen, "I want it to be open. It will look more spacious in here when that wall is no longer here. My brother keeps making plans to tear it down but some type of mishap always pops up. I think he thinks I am not going to pay him."

Richard looked as though he was willing to help. He looked the wall over, "It doesn't look like it will interfere with the structure. It actually looks like it was recently added. If you would like I could help. I know a few guys that do this type of work."

Crystal came in and smile showing her perfectly white teeth as she observed Richard and Brittany. Kierra and Jada didn't quite understand fully why Brittany never dated. Crystal knew it was all in her loyalty to the father of her child. She was really surprised that Brittany was even giving Richard the time of day.

"What you all needed some privacy?" Crystal asked being facetious but waiting on either of them to respond.

Richard walked over to Brittany and kissed her on the forehead. He headed back outside. Brittany was shocked. They had only hugged and held hands.

"What's that? Let me just guess. It's one of those I'll be loving you always the type of moments that Taye Diggs shared with Nia Long in the movie *The Best Man*." Crystal laughed.

"If you really want to know. I came in for some peace and quiet to accept Jarvis's call. Only to find out that he may be coming home soon." Brittany looked at Crystal in search of her coming to her aide with at least comforting her with some kind words or even a few that would be inspirational. There was a brief moment of silence. In walks, Jada and she had only heard part of the conversation. That didn't stop her though because each one of their face expressions let her know what the topic could be.

"Maybe if you let him get a little sample, you can show Jarvis that you, not a little girl anymore you are a woman. I know your hormones are raging out of control," Jada moved in closer to Brittany and placed her arm around her neck while resting her hand on Brittany's shoulder, "All you need is someone to hold you tight and fill up with that joy you need. Knock those darn cobwebs off that thang." Jada moved her hand toward the lower part of Brittany's body and patted in the area of her sexual organ. Brittany jumped back and Jada laughed, "I know you strictly dickly!" Jada laughed and headed back outside.

Crystal was couldn't hold it in. She busted it out with laughter, "That girl knows she is on one and y'all be trying to talk about me."

Brittany looked and Crystal and couldn't help but laugh. Crystal grabbed her hand and led her back outside. She leaned in towards to Brittany and whispered in her ear, "You know you need it. Don't be scared. Let that man touch and feel all on that poo nannie."

Chapter Thirteen

They got money for wars
But can't feed the poor.

Brittany was listening to Tupac's *Keep Yo Head Up* as she was getting ready for work. Six days after her birthday things in her love life had changed drastically. The last time she laid eyes on her son was on their birthday. She had talked to him every day. His grandparents were enjoying having him. They actually hoped and prayed that Brittany would only want to visit him. At this point where she was at in her life, which was all she intended on doing. She had spoken with her very own mother and she wasn't interested in rebuilding so Brittany was trying to really keep her head up. Her mother let her know that with the money that she received from the insurance she would share a portion with her. Her mother was trying to understand why she was concerned with rebuilding when her daughter had recently purchased her very own home. Brittany was going to be in search of finding some technicalities that stated that they only used the money could be to rebuild.

Brittany turned the volume up and continued to listen to Pac. Richard entered the room. He nodded his head to the beat taking in the serene picture as he watched Brittany having her own mini-concert. Brittany turned to grab the remote to turn the music down when she saw a familiar face on the television. The television was on mute. She was looking for the TV remote and Richard tossed it to her the remote.

The news reporter was talking to the aunt of Leslie Collins. The family was in search for some answers. The aunt looked at the camera and said, "Father, God, we need answers and we won't give up until we get them." They had increased the reward from five thousand to fifty thousand if anyone could provide any information on her whereabouts.

"I am surprised these little scramblers out here didn't come forward for the five thousand. I am curious to how these run off on the plug twice lil dudes respond to that fifty thousand." Richard said as he exited his bedroom.

Brittany looked at the time and realized that she had to be to work in two hours. After their little night cap, they fell asleep early and now she had been up with nothing to do. Richard was an early bird anyway. The last six mornings she had woke up and found him either working out or cooking breakfast. She headed to the bathroom to get ready. Brittany looked around and couldn't find her toothbrush.

She leaned her head out the bathroom and began to yell, "Richard, do you have an extra toothbrush. I can't find the one I left here yesterday."

"Look in the top drawer in the chest in my room. I forgot to tell you that I knocked it on the floor, so I threw it away."

Brittany walked back to the bedroom. She looked at his black lacquer wood grain chest and then towards the black lacquer wood grain armoire. Brittany didn't want to appear to be stupid but at the moment she didn't know the difference between the two. She walked over to the armoire. When she grabbed the handle she realized it was a door and not a drawer. As she opened she paused as she noticed the picture in the frame and then closed the door. She walked over to the chest in shocked. As she opened the top drawer she noticed a few toothbrush packs and grabbed one. She walked to the bathroom in total shock.

She stood in the mirror visualizing what she had just witnessed from the portrait in Richard's room. Brittany was trying to figure out what would be her next move. She was not about to keep holding in any more secrets. That one secret she was keeping from Jada was slowly tearing her apart. She added her new relationship she was having with Richard to her list. She was keeping that from her son and his father. Brittany was not about to add another secret that would begin to drain her mentally. She saw that one tear had escaped and ran down her face. She needed some answers. She thought about the barbershop conversation Crystal had told her about. Brittany hadn't asked Richard about his time in jail. She was caught up the pleasures he had been filling her up with. She felt as though she was in love. As she stood in the mirror she could see her heart breaking. She felt so betrayed. Brittany had the feeling as though she was about to throw up. She grabbed her stomach as the nostalgic feeling settled and dizziness set in. She sat down on the toilet trying to hold her head up. Brittany needed to think about her next move. She was so disappointed in herself. Every moment she and Richard had spent together the only spoke of the future. His past at the moment seemed so irrelevant. Brittany didn't know if he had kids or what he actually did as for as an income. All she knew was he worked out, he attended church regularly, drove a black Benz, lived alone, and had plenty of plans to be wealthy. She realized that she spent an enormous amount of time talking about her blog and her baby. But as she gathered herself and decided to confront him, she knew she had to choose her words wisely.

Brittany finished brushing her teeth and washing her face. She placed the toothbrush in the medicine cabinet. She took a deep breath and headed towards the kitchen. She pulled the stool out and took a seat. She rested her elbows on the granite countertop and watched his back as he stood over the stove scrambling eggs.

Brittany admired the muscles Richard put on display in his black wife beater as he stood over the stove. Brittany loved his relaxed look. He had to own over a thousand sweats but when he went out to handle business three-piece tailored suits was his choice.

Richard felt her presence. He turned around and grabbed the Waterford crystal glass pitcher filled with orange juice. He proceeded to fill her glass with orange juice. He prepared both their plates. Brittany smiled admiring the hash browns, turkey bacon, pancakes and scrambled eggs topped with American cheese.

They both bowed their heads and Richard began the prayer, "Gracious Lord, we give you thanks for the food prepared by loving hands that will nourish our bodies. We give thanks for this meal, life, and the freedom to enjoy it along with the other blessings that are yet to come. We pray for health and strength to carry on and strive to live as you would have us. This we ask in Jesus name."

"Amen." was said from the both of them in unison.

Brittany took a few bites. She thought about her words. Every time they had eaten he had blessed his food but they never had conversations about her returning to church. As she thought about it, he had never even mentioned any bible verses or had the come to Jesus type of conversations. She knew exactly how she would find out what she needed to find out, "So, how did you get so deep off in church."

Richard looked her directly in her eyes, "I made a promise to the Man above. In my life, I took all my losses like a man and promised Him if He got me out of this last situation I would honor him for the remainder of my days. My wrong and poor choices were redeemed due to His grace and mercy."

Brittany didn't expect him to be short and sweet with his response. She continued, "So, what was your last situation."

Richard appeared to be shocked. Brittany had never even really asked him much about himself. He really didn't know how to respond, "Don't you have to be at work soon?"

Brittany looked at the clock, "Yes, I do. My boss doesn't have a problem with me being a little late." Brittany knew she could call and let one of her friends know she would be late. Someone would cover for her need be. Just because she was getting her groove back, they were all excited for her. They would be waiting for her to come with some juicy details. Brittany raised one eyebrow and placed her hand under her chin. She let him know that he needed to come on with the details because she was not moving until he filled her in.

Richard really didn't want to relive the day he was arrested but the look Brittany was giving him let him know she was going to keep pressing until he gave her something. He wanted to lie but he knew the streets were talking. If she hadn't heard it she would eventually will. Richard took a deep breath, "Well in my hood I am known to most as Richie Rich. My uncle gave me the name because when I first started hustling I wouldn't buy anything. My homeboys would knock off their packages and hit the mall up. Me, I couldn't do that. My momma wasn't going for it. You could bring nothing in her house that she or my dad didn't buy. She didn't want to hear that it came from my friend. I respected that. So, I found me a spot in the basement of our house and hid my money. I was stacking it. Then came along this chic I was trying to get at. My uncle told me she was not seeing any little dusty boy. My uncle and I had this little game we'd play. I'd go shopping and drop my clothes off at his house. Then he would bring it to my house like he had bought them or someone gave them to him. Now fast-forward a little bit. I got the girl and I got heavy into the game. She and her mother were going to pick up the weight for me. We had a smooth little operation." Richard smiled thinking about how sweet he had it. He took a deep breath, "On their way back from Texas they stop to get gas. They stopped at the Mobil on Grand and Natural Bridge to get gas. While they went in to pay for some gas and getting something to drink. Some chic and her dude had beat up another chic. They pulled up to the gas station in the same identical car. A four-door gold Dodge Stratus. Both cars were empty. The police sat and waited for someone to come out. My girl's mother came out and started to pump the gas while they were watching. I wasn't there but I could only imagine what was going to those police minds. Two of the same cars and they were only after one. Well, the police went to the wrong car only looking for a gun and stumbled upon thirty pounds of heroin. I couldn't let her go to jail, so I turned myself in and said it was mine. The crazy thing is they didn't believe me. My name wasn't on any radars. I had stayed out the way for so long, there was no knowledge of me being connected to the streets. They were damn near about to throw the case out. They wanted her to give up the connect and being that she was a user with a record as long as my arm, they had a hard time believing she wasn't about to distribute it herself. They figured she was working for a major player due to her past. It was like a bunch of funny shit going on." Richard laughed thinking about the entire ordeal.

Brittany was looking at him like getting to the point with your story, please. For the most part, Richard didn't pay attention to her facial expressions like her friends. Brittany was thinking for the second time in her life she had put her trust in a man. First, it was Jarvis and he ran into a little mishap and left her to raise their son all alone. Now it was Richard. Part of the reason she was loyal to Jarvis was because she didn't want any other man to cause her any heartache. She couldn't express the feeling she was having at the moment with Richard. He hadn't cheated nor had he put his hands on her like Andre did Jada. Brittany was found herself being disappointed about his past. She was asking herself, why did she put her faith in a man and they failed her every time. This story he was reminiscing about had really confused her. He looked as though he was rekindling some sort of excitement about his past. Richard would smile as he hung on to every word that rolled off his tongue and his eyes were filled with ecstasy. She wanted to call him a buster so bad. Brittany let him continue.

"Her mother and I were both out but we were waiting to see what was going on with our case. A month later I went to see my boy Garland. I was telling him about what was going on with my case. He was scheming on his own shit. He started telling me about his cousin being in some dude's paperwork. Garland went on telling me about how he got a phone call and as soon as he hung up the phone call his house got kicked in. He said he felt like those folks were listening and the call gave them the break they needed with their case. Of course, the phone call had something to do with the business he was into." Richard thought about Denzel Washington's character Bumpy Johnson in the movie American Gangster, "I understand very well why Bumpy screamed and yelled, "Never on the phone!" Richard searched Brittany's face looking for some sort of approval. Brittany was listening but her focus was finding out about the photograph.

Richard continued, "We both thought it was somebody pulling a kick doe and he headed to grab his strap. The DEA came out from everywhere. Well, his dude was responsible for well over 1,000 federal and state narcotics law violations, as well as planning assassinations and concealing weapons. He told on about nineteen cats. The people was building a case for over two years. On the day they were dismantling a violent multi-national heroin trafficking organization operating in St. Louis, Missouri and Los Angeles, California, Fort Worth, Texas, and Mexico I happened to be sitting with one of the guys identified as a member of a high-level drug trafficking enterprise. One of the nineteen dudes had raped my girl's mother when she was a teenager. But, that's a whole other story. When she found out he was involved she gave his name and I got only seven years with the intent to distribute. I don't know how it happened but it did. While I was awaiting trial she was murdered. My girl went to live with her aunt. We lost touch during the fourth year I was down. I heard she lost the house we were staying in. It was like she just disappeared off the face of the Earth."

Brittany looked him in his eyes. The entire time he was speaking she felt as though she was listening to a Biggie Smalls meet the American Gangster Bumpy Johnson. Richard was giving here the watered down edited version of his life. Brittany wanted that the uncensored B.E.T. after hours' uncut version. Brittany settled for the moment due to the fact she did have to get to work. She could see the pain on his face and hear it as his voice began to tremble during the mention of the woman who he once loved. Richard went from being overly excited to someone down in the dumps. Not one time did he mention her name but Brittany knew who the girlfriend he was speaking about. She knew what she was getting ready to say was going to hurt him even more. Brittany was focused and was about to speak a few facts or ask some questions to get to the facts.

"So, you have increased the reward of fifty thousand to find her?" she searched for some answers as she held back to the truth. Brittany wanted to tell him she wasn't coming back but she could muster the strength. She sat a listened about his hustle but she didn't know the struggle. She didn't want any problems so she just kept her bit of information to herself. Brittany stood to embrace him. Richard hugged her back. Brittany kissed him on his forehead. She was mimicking his gesture he made every time they departed ways. Brittany was satisfied with what she had just heard. Crystal had heard a story that seemed to have gotten switched around by the time they were speaking on the matter in the barbershop. What Crystal overheard had been switched around. Richard was being blamed for what his girlfriend's mother had done. The version she repeated was watered down with a few truths. Brittany realized that Richard had been baptized by the streets and was trying to turn a new leaf. She was not going to crucify him just yet until he showed her different. Richard had been giving a new opportunity and life. His mistake didn't make him, it broke him and practically made him a new man. A new man that she would probably have to part ways with eventually. Jarvis was the only man in her life that would be allowed to be around her son.

Brittany finally made it to work. She knew that Kierra, Crystal, and Jada wanted to be filled in with Brittany's Richard chronicles. She was thinking about the story she was going to tell her friends. She didn't want to tell this hood star story which she sat and listened to. Brittany just knew they wanted to know what went on to make her so late for work. When she walked through the door they didn't ask her not one question. They did more of informing her on what they were doing while she was finding out Richard's past.

Kierra handed Brittany a piece of paper while Jada and Crystal were taking care of the customers. Brittany looked over the note Kierra had just handed her. The paper was titled the plan. It listed the money that was currently in the facility. Then it listed the projected amount of three million dollars for August. August was circled. Brittany couldn't even speak. Richard had just had her confused. Brittany's emotions were all over the place. She didn't know rather let him know that the girl he was looking for was never going to return. She was looking at Kierra and she wanted to tell her about the reward she could get and split if she'd plan on talking about it. She was fighting at all angles but she knew setting off the Check 'N Go was not going to be the big payback to it all.

Brittany gave the paper back to Kierra and retorted with sarcasm, "We need four million so it will be an even split. I can't believe that you all are really considering this." Brittany stood and placed herself in Kierra's proximity. She wanted to make sure that Kierra had a clear view of her face, "Kierra, what at about all your real estate plans. You know you can't start that Diamond in the Ruff organization from jail right?" Brittany moved into Crystal and pulled her sunglasses off, "She about to need rehab soon. I don't even know what drug she on. She goes from a nod to upbeat and perky personality. I would say she's doing meth but I've never been around it to know the symptoms. Jada is obsessed with some unknown dude that I saw kill Richard's girlfriend outside my bedroom window." Everything after that became a mumble. Brittany's brain was on overload. She had exploded with the bottled up information that was weighing her down. She had everyone's attention.

Jada hopped up from her seat and her smile turned upside down with frustration, "Hold the fuck up! Rewind! What the hell did you just say?" Jada voiced began to tremble as she moved closer to Brittany. She began pointing her finger in Brittany's face, "You mean to tell me you that you call yourself my friend and you didn't make me aware of none of this shit until you find yourself in this false fucking love triangle. Every time that you ever needed me I've always been there for you."

Brittany stood her ground, "Loose lips sink ships, Jada. I got rid of your phone to keep you from him. Now we all know damn well if I would have told you that you would not have thought rational about it. You would have found a way to ask him if it were true or not. Hell, he already killed Ms. Harris. Had he been free and amongst us ain't no telling the outcome would be of all of us. We told you to leave Andre a long time ago when we found out he was putting his hands on you. You didn't wake up to leave him until after spending the week in a coma. We still don't even know what happened or what he did that left you in a comatose state!"

Everyone looked at Brittany. They wanted to be mad at her. She had gone too far. Andre was a subject that they all came to an agreement to never mention. No one knew what to say. They all ignored the fact that she had mentioned Andre's abusive ass. Kierra and Crystal had a silly expression on their faces. Jada's face showed the hurt. Her eyes had begun to water. She ignored the last piece of the conversation. Jada acted as though she didn't hear it but her reaction was very different.

Brittany sat down and relived the night that Leslie was last seen. Brittany told detail for detail. She even went further in making the connection to Ms. Harris encounter of why she didn't fall down any steps. She brought them up to date with Richard and Leslie's relationship. Brittany felt as though the unnecessary load she was carrying was no longer. They all had forgiven Brittany in their heart for mentioning Andre. Jada, Kierra, and Crystal somehow felt that it was justifiable.

Crystal mumbled in her high daze, "J, she not lying about that. You like an old refrigerator. You can't keep shit!"

Kierra wanted to be mad at Brittany but she couldn't. She knew if Brittany would have shared any of that information with any of them things may have turned out different. Kierra was feeling quite sorry for Brittany. She appeared to be have carried a huge load. She only thought that Brittany was only backed up from being horny. She didn't know that the truth of the matter was she was carrying a huge load just trying to keep them all from danger.

Just as Jada was about to respond a tall dark dread head 2 Chainz impersonator entered the facility. The girls were all caught off guard. It was as if the mannequin challenge was taking place in the Check 'N Go and Bryson was the only one not participating. Jada moved to the window.

"Hey, you coming to cash a check?" Jada didn't know what to say.

Bryson smiled. He witnessed her nervousness. For second he intensified his problems. Bryson almost felt as though she was the reason he had spent a few weeks in jail. He knew that there was no way that she was connected but her vibe was telling him something else.

"What's up, Ma? Longtime no see! I have been to just about every Check 'N Go in this city looking for you. You changed your number on me. Then I go to your last known address and the entire building was gone. I looked around and in the next building, one of your old neighbors let me know that the building caught fire. The demolition came through and cleaned it up. Then I remembered you telling me where you worked. So, here I am!" Bryson stretched his arms out as if he were Kevin Hart thanking his fans for his stand-up performance at Philadelphia's Lincoln Financial Field.

Jada was afraid and she was hoping that Bryson had misread her look. He didn't. He knew something was going on but he didn't know what. He looked to the other girls and noticed that was the first time they had moved. Bryson asked Jada could she step outside and rap with him for a minute. She agreed. Crystal was no longer high. She pulled her sunglasses off and watched Jada walk to the door. Brittany and Kierra watch Jada make her exit as she was about to be executed. No one said a word. They all watched as Jada stood talking to Bryson. The situation had just got real. They didn't know what Jada would say about what had just taken place before he entered. They watched as they both took their cellphones out. Only about three minutes went by and Jada returned in the workplace.

"You all can quit looking stupid. I told him that I was in a committed relationship now. Bryson was actually cool with it. He told me he understood but he was going to try to win me over. He and I exchanged numbers. So, here I am." Jada took a deep breath, "I ain't gonna lie. It took everything in me not to ask him about the murder. He did ask me though why you all were acting so strange. I just told him that we were in here talking about robbing the place and you all probably think he heard us." Jada ended her spill very nonchalantly.

Brittany eyebrows raised in shock, "Why would you say that?"

Jada laughed, "Relax! I don't think he took me seriously. Besides, who the hell would he tell?"

Kierra jumped in, "The damn police!"

Jada looked at Kierra as if she were stupid, "The police really! He's a drug dealer and according to Brittany a murder. We know must criminals don't run to the police. They run from them!"

For a brief second, there was a moment of silence. The silence was broken with a burst of laughter coming first from Crystal. The Brittany and Kierra followed. Jada out laughed them all. The laughter derived from Jada's statement about Bryson being a murder but when they all noticed Crystal was no longer high, it intensified their laughter.

Each girl came in for a group hugged. They agreed to meet up after work and go out for drinks. Brittany let them know she would catch up with them later because she was going to visit with Jarvis for a while. They agreed on their location. As they were leaving work they didn't notice the 2 Chainz impersonator sitting in the midst of it all watching their every move. Kierra was the last one to leave. A phone call held her back. The store manager called to see if they were willing to work Saturday. Kierra knew everyone but Brittany would probably be willing to work. She couldn't remember if this was her weekend to go and visit Jarvis.

Kierra had a brief conversation with the ladies that came in after them. She noticed they were working short one worker. Kierra checked with Charlise, the shift manager during the next shift, to see if she would be okay. Charlise let her know that if she needed her she would reach out to her. Kierra let her know it wasn't a problem and she then left the workplace.

Kierra entered her car and let all the windows down. She was trying to let all of the St. Louis heat that was bottled up in her car for the last eight hours' escape. She had the air on high hoping and praying it was going to cool off quick. Before she let the windows back up she adjusted her radio. The sound of John Coltrane's *A Summer Love* had instantly intensified her heartbeat. She could feel the emotion and spirituality that Coltrane was conveying in this piece. A delusion of success set in as she took off from the parking lot of her workplace. She bobbed her head to the melodic tunes and smiled at the pedestrians who were in the insane heat moving about as though they were a part of the rat race which was taking place. As she continued to drive and let the smooth sounds of Coltrane take control she came to an abrupt stop as a black Monte Carlo darted in front of her. She gathered herself, turned her music down, looked around to ensure herself the coast was clear and she continued to drive. Kierra couldn't remember where they had agreed to meet up so she searched for her cell phone to call one of the girls. As she was about to place her call she noticed that Dominque was calling her. She turned the radio completely off before she answered.

"Hey, babe!" Kierra said as she pressed answered and lifted the phone to her ear.

"What's up, Kierra? I was calling to see if you had any plans tonight. We got an unexpected call and were ask to play at the Signature Room tonight. The show will start about ten." Dominique informed her.

"Of course, I'd be there. My girls and I are going out to eat. I am sure they would be down to come out and support. I will see you at the Signature Room at ten." Kierra ended the call. She knew she had to call Brittany. She was hoping that if she were still at Jarvis's parent's house she could convince them to go to his visit so that Brittany could work, if this were the weekend she was supposed to visit him. Kierra made the call just in time Brittany was about to walk out the door when the call came through. She let Kierra know she would call her back once she found out. Brittany didn't want Jarvis to not have a visit. She was currently feeling as though he knew she was seeing someone. She didn't want to go and sit with him and have Richard running across her mind. She didn't know how she would react in Jarvis's presence. She felt so shamefaced starting a new relationship and guiltier from hiding it from Jarvis. She somehow felt that she was protecting him from her infidelity. Brittany hadn't heard from him since her and Jarvis, Jr. birthday. Brittany called Kierra back and let her know that everything was cool. His parents had agreed to make the visit. She was cool going to see him but after she and Richard had been intimate the feeling had changed.

Chapter Fourteen

The Check 'N Go was the quietest it had ever been on a Saturday morning. They hadn't worked a Saturday since they had been employed at the check cashing place. The girls enjoyed their Friday night which consisted of dinner and dancing. The time appeared to be moving so slow. Brittany could barely keep her eyes open. She kept checking her phone to see if Jarvis had called. She knew his parents had explained to him that she received a last minute notice to work. While she was waiting she decided to text Richard. A couple of exchanges led to another outing. She let him know that she would meet him at his place around seven. They had only had a brief conversation since the morning he had given her an edited version of his big fame and prestigious street status he formerly had. Although she was thinking about Richard, Brittany really wanted to talk to Jarvis and find out about this release he was expecting. She couldn't go against him and ask his parents for any updates. She wasn't really sure if he had even shared the news with his parents. The few times she had been around his parents they never even mentioned Jarvis. His parents really didn't know that Brittany and Jarvis considered themselves being in a committed relationship.

Jada was scrolling down her Facebook timeline. Crystal looked over her shoulder and noticed that she was lurking Bryson's page. She came across a picture came across a picture with Bryson and Danitra. Jada realized it had to be old due to the fact that his dreads weren't as long as they were when she met him. Jada looked back at Crystal to see if she had peeped what she had just noticed. Crystal tapped Jada on the shoulder and grabbed her phone. Crystal took a few steps with Jada in tow. Crystal placed the phone in front of Brittany. The look on Brittany's face was priceless. It was though her eyes were flashing as if it were an ambulance or police cruiser.

Brittany took her eyes off the picture, "Have you talked to him?"

Jada wanted to be truthful. She knew that she needed to be. That was the issue she and her friends were having. They need to be more open and honest with one another. She had been talking on the phone with Bryson every day since he left from coming up to her job after he had been released from jail. She just hadn't seen him. She knew she couldn't take too long answering the question. Jada needed to answer and she needed to answer fast. She hadn't asked him anything about the murder but she knew her friends wouldn't believe her. "He old news. He has text me a few times. I prolly replied once or twice. It wasn't anything but that when can I see you text. I wanted to reply, I am a scary broad and I don't mess around with killers. I refrained. I just told him I was working on some etches I was trying to get ready for this fashion show I have been invited to." Jada felt really good about her response. She didn't know rather they fell for it or not. She really didn't care but she wanted to reassure them that she would never inquire about the killing Bryson had allegedly taken place in. Jada was being partially honest. She was telling Bryson lies about what she had going on in her life. She was trying to impress him with her future plans. Jada just wasn't doing the etches for an upcoming fashion show like she claimed to Bryson she was doing.

Crystal gave Brittany that's that bullshit look. Then they shared a laugh. Jada wanted to ask what was funny but she decided against it. They made a vow not to bring Andre's name up and the vow had been broken. Andre was a touchy subject for her. Jada was going to avoid the risk of hearing his name again. She knew exactly why they were laughing. They either didn't believe the lie she just told or it was worthy to be believed with some stretched truth. Jada just left them to have their moment.

Brittany handed Jada back her phone. As she handed her the cell phone she looked at Crystal and said, "I should call Danitra and see what she has been up to lately."

As Crystal leaned back in the black swivel barstool she placed her arms on the armrest. She then looked over at Jada who was on her right then back towards Brittany which was on her left, "Nope! Just let her be. She has your number and if she really wanted to get in touch with you, she would have called you by now. The real question is," Crystal paused and took a deep breath, "what are you going to do with this information you have? Are you going to tell Richard what you think you know? Will you just hold this until the right opportunity come along and present itself? I guess what I really want to know is, what's your plan?"

"Damn!" Kierra yelled interrupting the others conversation. The check cashing business was quite slow for a Saturday. She had waited on a few customers and during the down time she was scrolling down her timeline. The girls all turned in her direction looking and waiting on what had excited her. She stood up with her cellphone in hand. She showed the girls a picture of a young man looking as though he was lying in a puddle of blood in the middle of the street. The young man was wearing a white t-shirt and some khaki shorts.

"Damn!" Crystal yelled with tears rolling down her face. I wonder where that is. That's messed up. Someone's child just lying out there in the street.

Kierra continued to scroll the Facebook page. The next picture popped up was identical to the first. This one just displayed an officer standing off looking over the dead body. Brittany walked towards the back to turn on the television. She went directly to the news channel stations. There was nothing on the television reporting the incident. They now were all on their phone scrolling. Within seconds the sounds of sirens and police cars speeding past the check cashing place led them to believe the crime scene wasn't too far from them.

Jada came across a video on her timeline. There were a few people talking about how the police didn't have any reason to shoot the boy. The guy was saying it was a dead body just lying in the street. There were several conversations taking place that could be overheard in the video. Several obscenities were being yelled out at the crime scene. The homicide had made it to the scene and had begun tape off the scene. In seconds they could see a man running up to the body and the police had stopped him in his tracks. The guy that was recording was telling someone that he heard that the guy had his hands up while the police were shooting. He repeated over and over saying how dirty the cops were. The video they were watching came to an end.

Kierra came across another video. Kierra watched as the others listen to the guy as he said, "He was on the ground and they still shot'em. They were really trying to get at dude. He had his hands up and everything. That's his daddy over there. His dad just ran up but the police stopped him. That's his aunt standing over there in the scrubs. That's fucked up Dog. Those some lousy mother fuckers. They shot the boy while he was down on the ground. Police just killed the dude. He had his hands up and everything. They just got him just lying in the street dead as a mother fucker. This shit is unreal. I thought it was another nigga dumping on him or something. I didn't see anybody but the police. This fucked up. Why the do this shit to us? Why haven't they even covered him up yet?" They listened to the person as he talked and aimed his phone at the body of the young man who was dead in the middle of the street.

You could hear other people yelling in the background, "Call the ambulance!" Other spectators start asking about the young man's hat. They were trying to figure out what was going on and why the young man was still lying in the street. The video Kierra was playing and showing on her phone had ended.

Brittany came across another video. They were under the assumption that it was the mother that had made it to the scene. She was yelling and someone was telling her about how many shots they had heard. She had begun to scream asking why. The way she was grieving gave them further confirmation that she was the victim's mother.

Jada walked back to the television. She was searching through all the channels, "Why this stuff not on the news? This is crazy. Where are all those damn news reporters now? I am quite sure those scanners had picked up this incident." More police were speeding by the check cashing place.

They continued to scroll down their timelines. Kierra came across a picture. She walked over to Brittany, "Look who was out there? I guess this must have happened over there where he stays."

Brittany grabbed her phone and began to call her brother. She listened to his cell phone ring and it went to his voicemail after several rings. "Brandon, call me as soon as you get this message. I need to know if you are okay." She dialed him right back.

Jada tapped Brittany on her shoulder. They walked over to the television and watched as her brother was reporting about the incident they had just watched on social media.

Brandon began by saying, "We were walking down the street the middle of the street. We were not causing any problems. We didn't have any weapons. No cars were blowing at us. Then the officer pulled up and told us to get the fuck out of the street. We let him know we were almost at our destination and we were just having a conversation. He pulled away for about a few seconds and then he bagged back in a way where it almost hit us. His squad car was now blocking the street. He pushed his door open real fast and it swung back. The door swinging back caused him to look like he was in a rage. He then reached out the window and grabbed my friend by the neck. The officer was trying to pull him in the car. My friend was trying to get away. The officer then pulled his gun and told my friend he was going to shot. Well, a few seconds later the officer shot his gun. We both saw blood and we both began to run. My friend told me to run one way as he ran another way. The officer was in pursuit of my friend. I ran and ducked behind a car because I feared for my life. I could still see that my friend was running from the officer. The officer then shot him again. My friend stopped running and turned around with his hands up. The officer continued to shoot. Then I noticed that my friend had died." The interview was over and the station had gone to commercial. Jada changed the channel to see if anyone else was reporting the shooting. Brittany's cell phone rang. It was Brandon. She immediately answered the phone, "Are you okay?" her tears began pouring down her face. Jada stood by her rubbing her back as she tried to comfort her.

Brandon was huffing and puffing, "Where are you?"

"I am at work. Do you need me to come get you?"

"I need to go to your house and just chill. It's crazy out here. I am getting ready to get someone to bring me up there. Can you leave so we can go to your spot?" Brandon inquired.

"You know it's all good. We can leave when you get here." Brittany assured him and ended their call.

Jada didn't wait on Brittany tell let them know what had happened. She couldn't wait, "What he say, B?"

"He is on his way up here. We are about to go to the house so he can relax. I am just glad he's okay." Brittany sat down and held her head within her hands.

Brittany phone began to ring like crazy. Danitra was the first person to reach out to her. Jarvis parents had even called her. The only phone call she answered was her aunt. She was worked up and didn't want to talk to anyone. She let her aunt know that she would have Brandon call her as soon as they made it to the house. Brittany hated the fact that a family had to bury their child. She was thankful that it wasn't their family being faced with the tragedy. Brittany would never say that allowed because she didn't to want to sound selfish or heartless. Within moments Brandon walked through the Check 'N Go doors. All the girls exited through the door, to enter the lobby, to greet him at the door. They said their goodbyes and Jada let them know she would see them at the house later. Brittany knew everyone would be there once they got off from work.

The ride home was quiet. It was hard for Brittany not to ask him any questions. She embodied the feeling she had on the day they were taken from their mother. She knew he would talk when he was ready. The entire drive he sat just looking out the window. Before they made it to the house the only thing he asked did she everything he needed for him to knock the wall down. She lived ten minutes from her job but this drive seemed as though they were walking the green mile. She pulled up at the house. They entered and Brandon immediately began to close all the doors, cover the furniture and hang plastic. He did that so the dust from him knocking down the wall wouldn't be all over everything.

Brittany went to her bedroom to call her aunt to let her know that Brandon was with her and he was fine. Their aunt told Brittany to tell Brandon to call her when he felt like talking. Brittany agreed and then called Jarvis's mom. They talked about the visit and Brittany found that her son was okay. He was happy that he had seen his dad. She let her go when Brandon banging began to get louder. When she no longer heard the banging she exited her room. She could not believe what she was witnessing. Brandon was pulling money wrapped in plastic from inside the wall. Brittany turned around and walked back to her bedroom. She came back with a black duffle bag. No one said a word. Together they removed the money and stuffed it in the bag. Once the bag was filled Brittany took it to her bedroom and put it in her closet. She began to help Brandon take the drywall to the trash. It was a small built wall filled with several stacks of money.

On their last trip to the trash, Brandon finally spoke, "I am going to clean this up and add a piece of trim. So, when are you going to count that money?" Brandon was anxious. He was willing to let Brittany handle what she needed to handled but he wanted a cut.

Brittany looked at Brandon, "I am going to count it when Jada is not about to walk through the door at any moment. Don't get me wrong. I am going to kick her down with a few stacks. I am even going to break bread with Kierra and Crystal. I just need to see what's what." Brittany didn't want to start talking about finding out who the money belonged to. Brittany knew she hadn't put it there and whoever may have built the wall just may still be around to come and confiscate it back. If confronted she was going to act like she didn't know anything about anything. She knew she could tell them that she had just moved there but the problem was how willing were they to listen to her plead her case.

Brandon in returned said, "Yea, keep that to yourself for a moment. You may have to pay for me a lawyer."

"Why would you need a lawyer? You didn't do anything. Are you ready to tell me what all happened?"

Brandon began to pull the plastic down. Brittany laughed. She had been waiting for him to knock that small portion of the wall down and it took him all of an hour to knock it down, frame it off and clean it up. All he needed to do was paint the area in which he had framed off.

Brandon grabbed him a bottled water from the refrigerator and took a deep breath, "Last night Mitchell came and knocked on my door. He a wanted to fire up. I told him I was chilling with my gal and my baby. I let him know that when I woke up in the morning I would come get him. Mitchell left and I chilled. When I woke up that morning I went to get him. I knocked on the door. He let me know he didn't have any cigarillos. We headed to go get some. As we were walking he was telling me how the world was going to know his name. You know he was working on a mixtape and he was talking about his plans. When we made it to the main street he did something real strange." Brandon paused.

Brittany didn't say a word. She wanted him to get to the point and finish the story. She wanted to know why her brother felt as though he was going to need a lawyer. She was not about to interrupt him. When he was done with his pause he continued on to tell her his account of the tragedy that was being spread like a wildfire on the internet.

"You know the street we were about to cross stays busy. Mitchell reached out to me. He placed his hand on my chest and told me not to look. Mitchell told me to put my faith in him. He was going to get us across the street. Now you know this a four lane street and some fools thinks it a highway. We got across the traffic that was going north and made it to the middle of the street. I felt like an umpire at a baseball game. I wanted to yell out safe when we made it to the middle of the intersection. Now we had to make it pass the traffic that was going south. I got ready to look to make sure the coast was clear and he reached out to me again. He told me that he had me and I needed to keep my faith with him. Mitchell wasn't even looking at me. He was looking straight ahead. Not one time did he check for traffic! We just walked across the street. I was scared as that deal."

Brittany couldn't resist, "Wait! Hold up. Who does he think he is? You sure he wasn't already high?" Brittany chuckled. She felt bad when her brother looked at her as if she was stupid.

114

"B, he was freaking me out. It was like a spiritual warfare was taking place within him. On one side the devil was trying to rise but Jesus was superseding the entire ordeal. We made across the street and walking towards Ferguson Market. We walked in the store and he was on some DEBO type of trip. He had tripped me out from crossing the street that I wasn't even focused while we were in the store. He was trying to tell the man in the store he didn't have his Id. He was like you know me. I come in here all the time. You don't ask me for identification any other time. He grabbed a few cigarillos and we were out."

Brittany interrupted, "Y'all didn't pay for the cigarillos?"

"Nope, so when the cop pulled up I knew it wasn't due to the store owner calling the police. You know we wouldn't have made it across the street. We were almost at my spot by the time the cop rolled up on us." Brandon took a drink of his bottle watered that he had been holding, "Dude pulled up and was like get the fuck out the street. Mitchell ignored him but I spoke up. I was like officer we are almost at our destination we will be out the street in a few minutes. I don't know what happened next. It was like those demons that were in Mitchell hopped off him and onto the cop. He bagged back in a hurry and almost hit us. He was on Mitchell's side so he reached out to grab him. He was holding him by the neck. Mitchell got away from his hold and then dude pulled his strap. The officer started talking real reckless. Next thing I know he shot and we both saw blood. It was like the cop had no control and became scared. We didn't know what to do but Mitchell yelled out run. He and I both start running. The cop began to chase Mitchell. He was dumping at him the entire time he was running. As the cop was firing his weapon nonstop, it was like Mitchell felt the need to give up. He stopped running and he turned around with his hands up. It was like he was walking towards the cop in slow motion with his hands up. Then he fell. The cop stood over him and shot him a few more times. I was hiding behind this black Monte Carlo watching as the cop shot him in cold blood. It was some dude and a girl smoking a blunt. They saw the entire thing. Old boy got out the car and was asking me what had happened." Brandon was trying to hold back his tears. He was looking as though he was lost.

Brittany looked at her brother, "I am glad you are okay but I know his parents fucked up behind this. That's crazy. How did the dude look that was in the Monte Carlo?"

Brandon laughed, "You know what's even crazy. When I saw the dude I thought I was tripping. Dude look just like 2 Chainz. On some real shit, I thought it was him for a second. When he started rapping with me, I knew it wasn't him. He had me for a second, though. Enough about that. What are we going to do about that money?" Brandon looked over at the door as the doorknob was turning. He didn't say anything else about the money.

Jada, Kierra, and Crystal came through the door. They began talking about how fast he had knocked the wall down. Jada had to let him know he could have completed that project a long time ago. Brittany went into the kitchen to make some Ro-Tel dip. Her friends were doing their rendition of either The View or The Talk. They were asking her brother a million and one questions. He was telling them the same story he had just finished telling his sister.

When Brittany finished with the meal and they all had eaten Brandon told her that he may need to go home. He had left his family and he didn't know how that was about to pan out. Brandon didn't want his child nor the mother of his child in an odd situation. They all agreed. Jada suggested she would go get them and they could just come there. Kierra let them know that wasn't a good idea. Kierra continued by telling him that his absences made him appear to be guilty. The talked a few minutes and they all got in Jada's truck to drop him off.

When they made it to his apartment complex there was a crowd of people standing out there. The body was gone but there were over a hundred of people surrounding the area where a body was

116

recently laid out in the street. The body was no longer. It had been replaced with several candles and teddy bears. There was traffic but it moved slowly through the crowd. Brandon's apartment building was two parking lots away from the crime scene. He was far enough where he couldn't look out the window to see the people. But, he was close enough to hear the crowd chanting hands up, don't shoot and black lives matter.

Brandon exited Jada's truck. Kierra, Crystal, Brittany and even Jada watched him as he entered the apartment. Brittany decided to follow just so she could go in and see her niece. Jada soon followed. She knocked on the door to see the baby as well. Before they knew it all four girls were in the apartment giving Brandon's baby all their attention. A few minutes later, Brandon, Jada, and Crystal were sitting at his kitchen table blazing a blunt. Brandon's baby mother, Demeasha, had gone to her bedroom. She was not the social type. She had the attitude that many women had when it comes to men and their family. She felt as though she only had dealings with her man and she didn't have to deal with his family. She was there for him and only him. Brandon didn't let her attitude bother him. He knew that she loved him. While her apartment was filled with a few women she had heard of, she was not trying to get to know any of them.

Once they were done smoking they decided to leave. As they were leaving the complex the people that were out there had doubled. It took them all of an hour to exit a route that wasn't even two minutes long. They observed a crowd of people. Some were angry, while others were crying but they were all in support of each other to help overcome what appeared to be a difficult time. The car ride was quiet. Jada had to keep her eyes on the road. Darkness began to fall as they were trying to make their escape. She was ensuring all their safety as they observed all those that were hanging out in the apartment complex. When they made it to the main intersection Jada made a right turn. They rode passed their place of employment and headed to the store. Jada and Crystal had been made plans to go to Walmart and get a few duffle bags. Since they were out that way Jada felt as if it were no time like the present to make that happen.

Jada pulled on Walmart's parking lot and parked. She and Crystal went in the store. Kierra and Brittany were left in the car. They sat in silence. Kierra had counted the people that had entered the store and came out before Jada and Crystal. She saw a familiar face. Kierra tapped Brittany on the shoulder to get her attention. They watched as Bryson had entered the Walmart.

"How the fuck does he do that?" Kierra asked.

"Does what?" Brittany inquired.

"I swear that nigga has to be Harry Houdini. He just pops up when you least expect it. I don't want to hear that mess St. Louis ain't but this big. I have been here my whole life and my parents are out here. I have never bumped into them nowhere out here." Kierra popped her lips.

"Well, hopefully, he and Jada don't see each other while they are at Walmart," Brittany said as she watched Crystal and Jada exit the Walmart. She continued, "It's funny you said that. I think Brandon was hiding behind his car. Brandon told me that as he hid behind the black Monte Carlo some 2 Chainz looking dude got out the car. I thought that was crazy. That dude is everywhere." Brittany couldn't help to think about when she first came in indirect contact with Bryson.

Kierra watched as Jada and Crystal approached the truck. Before the door opened she was able to tell Brittany not to say anything about Bryson. Wait to see if they would bring it up.

Brittany watched as they entered the truck with what looked to be about four duffle bags, "What the hell are you all about to do?" Brittany had a feeling about what the bags were for. She was just trying to figure out why they needed those bags while she was with them.

Jada just looked at Brittany as if she were stupid.

"What's the look for. Hell, why can't you just tell me what you are up to because how you are acting is confusing me!" Brittany raised her voice and the irritation could be felt. Brittany was not about to let anyone jeopardize her freedom.

Jada just pulled off the lot and continued to drive as if Brittany had not said one word to her. As they made it down the road near Brandon's apartment complex they could see a crowd of people walking towards the QT. Jada pulled on the lot and went in to purchase a dollar worth of gas. As Jada exited the QT, Crystal exited the truck with the gas can. Crystal filled the gas can and placed it in one of the empty Walmart bags. She then placed the gas can in the back of the truck. They sat in the truck and watched several people enter the QT. One guy began to spray paint the building with a blurb that stated, snitches get stitches. Others began running in and just stealing things. The QT workers disappeared before their eyes. The people were left all alone to ransack the store.

Jada, Brittany, Crystal and Kierra couldn't believe what they were witnessing. As soon as a kid started firing a Roman candle firework, Jada managed to get them off the lot. Jada was headed to the Check 'N Go. As they approached they could see the Brinks truck alone with their boss in the distance. Jada slowed down giving them both a chance to pull off. They didn't take any time leaving because they could see the crowd pouring into the streets. Jada was able to pull right up to the Check 'N Go. Kierra made her exit with her keys. She unlocked the door and headed straight to the steel door to disable the alarm. Kierra waved her hand to signal for her girls. Jada and Crystal followed with the duffle bags.

Brittany sat in the car in disbelief. She knew what they were going in there to do. She was trying to figure out when they came to the conclusion to actually follow through with robbery. Brittany was thinking about the alarm and the alarm company. She was trying to figure out how was this going to fly. When they came to work in the morning how were they going to maintain a straight face. She was trying to conjure up a story tell. She anticipated the worse. For a brief moment, Brittany had a vision of herself wearing Missouri Department of Corrections gear.

"These broads about to really set it off." Brittany laughed, "I can't believe these broads." Brittany looked around to see if anyone was looking. All the action was taking place about fifty yards from them. Then there was a loud boom. Brittany jumped. The entire QT was engulfed in flames. This situation instantly became confusing. She was feeling as though she was in a dimension unknown to man. There was a brief feeling of improbability. She snapped out of it when she looked up and saw the two security cameras on the building. One was only for show and the other one actually recorded. That was the one that zoomed in and out on the entry way to the check cashing place. Brittany exited the truck and walked straight to the back. When she went to remove the tape, it wasn't there. Brittany was confused about the missing tape. She unhooked the equipment and took the entire surveillance equipment. Brittany watched as Jada, Kierra, and Crystal was stuffing the duffle bags with stacks of cash.

"B, I need you to go get that gas can," Crystal said to her not taking her eyes off the cash she was expeditiously putting in the bag.

Brittany walked right outside and came back in with the gas can. She began to sprinkle the liquid from the entry way all the way to back door exit that was never used.

Jada walked out first. She looked around. There was no one at the storage unit that was next to the Check 'N Go. All the action was taken place across the street to her left. The QT was at an angle from where she was standing. She had stood there on several occasions puffing on a Newport. Jada would watch people pull on or off the QT parking lot while she was puffing on her cigarette. Today she was standing with two duffle bags full of money. She thought about how she had parked. Jada placed the bags back in the building. Jada had to be sure she didn't sit them in the gasoline. She entered her truck. As she started it up she was evaluating how she was about to turn it around and back it up to the door. She completed that task in under a minute. Jada didn't have to get back out of her truck. Her partners in crime were stuffing the bags in the back of the truck. Brittany and Kierra entered the truck. They both looked around checking out their surroundings. Crystal had sat the paper for a wire transfer on fire.

Brittany looked back and seen the flame as Crystal walked briskly to enter the truck. She exhaled, "I've had my share of fires for my lifetime. I am getting an electric stove so I can eliminate seeing flames from here on out."

Police sirens began to sound. If it were not for the crowd that had begun to bombard the street, they would have become nervous. There were several businesses burning. Jada drove in slow motion. A St. Louis County officer was clearing the street. Jada let him lead the way. In ten minutes they were pulling on to her and Brittany's street. There was a parking space directly in front of their home. She pulled right in. It was so quiet in the car the only thing you could hear were their heartbeats. Jada turned the car off and turned her body where she could see everyone's face. She began to yell and beat her seat. Crystal joined her in the screaming match. Kierra smiled as she looked at her girls and Brittany had covered her eyes with her hands. Each one of them was filled with excitement.

"Okay. We are just going to get out the truck and sit on the porch. We are going to look at everything and everyone on this street. We are going to agree that the coast is clear before we take the bags out the truck." Brittany said as she tried to think rationally.

They exited the truck and all took their respective places on the steps. The darkness interfered with a portion of the view as the street lights brightened other portions. A few seconds out there they noticed a black Monte Carlo bend the corner. The car drove down the street and slowed down. They watched as the driver slowly lowered the driver side window. Bryson smiled with a devious look.

"Girl, I am not about to keep stalking" Bryson waited on a response.

Each one of them sat there speechless. They didn't know what to expect. Brittany stood up and turned her back towards Bryson, "I am about to call Richard." Brittany pulled out her door key from out her pocket and unlocked the door.

"I'll go with you." Kierra stood up to follow Brittany, "you give me the damn keys to the truck and watch my mother fucking money." Kierra grabbed the keys from Jada and chirped the alarm. She left Crystal and Jada on the porch to entertain Bryson.

Teresa Seals

Chapter Fifteen

You have a collect call from, Jarvis. An inmate in Southeast Correctional facility. This call is subject to be recorded. To accept the charges, dial eight. To deny the charges dial nine.

"Damn! This is Jarvis. I don't really want to talk to him right now. But, I need to. I have not spoken with him since my birthday and not going to see him yesterday was kind of hard for me. I have never missed a visit since he has been down." Brittany had answered the phone in such a hurry that she didn't pay attention to the number. She felt the phone as it vibrated and pressed answer. She knew she needed to hurry up and press eight. The recording had repeated itself for the third time. She quickly pressed eight.

Brittany waited for the call to be connected. As soon as she could hear the background she began to speak, "Sorry about that. I had to dry my hands." Brittany lied.

Kierra walked over to the front window to see what was going on outside with Jada, Crystal, and Bryson. She was actually making sure the truck was outside and was not being tampered with. She then went to the front door to lock it. She was having an eerie feeling. Kierra walked back over to the window and made it obvious she was watching. Bryson had parked and was now standing on the sidewalk with Jada and Crystal not too far from the truck. The ghetto Olympics was currently in effect. The blunt relay was going down as Kierra was trying to figure out how this clown just conveniently showed up in places where they could be found. Her gut feeling was telling her something was not right about Bryson. Even though Brittany made them all aware that he wasn't the average person they had usually surrounded themselves amongst, Kierra had weird unexplainable feelings about Bryson. She was fighting with the feeling of calling the authorities and making them aware of his involvement in the abduction of Leslie Collins. Then she thought about what proof she had. She nor Brittany had any proof. As she stood in the window observing his demeanor, she thought about how things would have been different if Brittany had the opportunity to take his picture when she went to grab her phone that night. Kierra stood watching Bryson as he entertained her friends. He avoided making eye contact. He would look in her direction every now and then. But, he kept his focus on the two women he was smoking the blunt with at the time.

Jarvis had called to find out what was going on with Brandon. The news had traveled two hours and a half away. Jarvis was trying to make sure his family back home was okay. He knew it wasn't much he could do. Letting them know he was concerned and he hearing that everyone was fine put him at ease. Brittany clicked over to call Brandon while she and Jarvis were on the phone. As she and Jarvis were on the phone checking up on Brandon, he let them know that so many news outlets had contacted him. They were trying to set up interviews to get his accounts of what took place at his apartment complex. Brandon was watching television as he spoke on the phone. Jarvis wasn't providing him with any new information. He was flipping through the channels seeing his face on just about every network. To top it off his phone had been ringing constantly. Every journalist from near and far was trying to speak with him. Brandon eventually stopped answering his phone. He couldn't believe what he was witnessing. The city was on fire. The people were looting and rioting. He was too scared to close his eyes because all he could see when they were closed were Mitchell Crawford being slaughtered in the middle of the street for no reason at all.

Kierra listened as Brittany talked to Jarvis. She took out her phone and start scrolling down her timeline. She came across a video that was titled *We Love You Leslie*. Kierra clicked on the video and recognized the lady as Leslie's aunt. This woman was not giving up in her quest to find her niece. Kierra listened as the lady spoke.

We are still looking and praying that Leslie makes it home safely. Today we are going to canvass the areas of Berkley, Ferguson, and Pagedale. We have a feeling those are the areas Leslie was last seen. Our family truly misses her. This has been a struggle trying to hold it together. I know someone knows something. Please contact the police department. I thank you all for sharing my videos. We all are concerned and sad. Her family is not going to stop until will find her. We are working with the police to bring our loved on back. There are too many young girls missing and no one is saying anything. It time people speak up. These people who are behind these crimes are only continuing because no one will speak up. The minute we began to speak up, this mess may stop. We must put their images out there because someone knows something. Your efforts are not in vain. I thank everybody who is assisting us in our efforts.

The woman spoke with strength and courage. It was very obvious she had been crying and was now holding back her tears. She held a picture up of Leslie as the video came to an end. Kierra was frantic. She was almost brought to tears. She knew it was something that could be done but she just didn't know what. Kierra was standing in the window feeling real antsy. She was trying to figure out why she was the only one having major panic attacks about Leslie's allegedly abduction. Kierra wanted to count the money and put it up. She wanted to call the police or even contact Leslie's family. She just stood with there while her emotions were running wild as she looked out the window with disgust. Bryson was too close to her piece of the dream. He had already robbed one person of their dreams. Kierra didn't want to be his next victim. She envisioned all of the investments she was about to make and then it went all up in smoke as she saw Bryson destroying her vision.

Brittany was on the phone observing Kierra. She could overhear the video but she couldn't make out what was being said because she was still on the phone with Jarvis and Brandon listening to their conversation. Brittany watched as Kierra was experiencing several emotions. She took it as though Kierra was just anxious about the money in the truck. Jarvis let Brittany know that he would call her back and let her know the results of his hearing. He let her know that his caseworker informed him that the parole board was impressed with his behavior and his teaching of several classes like anger management. The call ended without either one of them saying goodbye. They had ignored the minute reminder warning. She told Brandon that she would talk to him later and the call came to an end.

Brittany looked through her call log and searched for Richard's name. She found his name and tapped on it.

"Speak on it." This was Richard's response as he answered his phone. He spoke like the boss he once was.

"Hello? Richard?" Brittany was confused. She didn't know if someone else answered his phone or if the wires were somehow crossed. She felt the demand for respect come from those three words. Speak on it had her lose her train of thought. Brittany was turned on from his tone.

"This me, girl. I was just fooling around with you. I am at church and I am feeling a really good. What's up with you?" Richard asked in such a seductive manner. His boss tone quickly changed to the voice you loved to hear in the bedroom. It was not smooth and seductive.

"Are you busy? I would like to speak with you about something." Brittany waited on him to respond. She was hoping the gangster she just witnessed through the phone showed back up.

"I am at this church revival right now. I was actually planning on calling you to see what you were up to tonight. Now I don't have to because you called me." Richard blushed. He went from gangster to Romeo real quick. Richard was really feeling Brittany. She wasn't like most of the females he encountered. He dealt with women of a different caliber. Brittany was eight years younger than him but her maturity was equivalent to his. He respected her for that. Richard saw Brittany as a classy and calm woman who was very independent. She didn't have her hand out like the needy women who flaunted and flocked towards him. Everyone that was coming for him was looking for Richie Rich. The man who was one the king of St. Louis. Brittany didn't' care about who the man he once was. She was more interested in how he treated her and the man he had become. They both were enjoying each other's camaraderie. Richard couldn't believe that he hadn't been intimate with her. This was the first time he had ever experienced that. Richard was hoping she wasn't on that Steve Harvey's *Think Like A Man* ninety-day rule. He didn't know how to take that if she was but it didn't matter to him at the moment. Any other time women were throwing their drawers at him and couldn't resist the thought of him throwing them a few dollars.

"When you leave church can you come by here? I have some things I would like to discuss with you and I'd rather not discuss it over the phone." Brittany waited for his response.

Richard was pleased but yet a tad bit shocked. He didn't even know how to respond. He and Brittany had been kicking it for almost four months. Richard had only been invited to her house once and that was on her birthday. He felt that he had paused too long and decided to speak, "Sure! I will be by there as soon as I am done here."

"Okay. See you then." Brittany ended the call, "I know he used to be heavy in the streets and unless that church thang putting money in his pocket, he either still in the game or he retired at the pinnacle of the game." Brittany joined Kierra in the window. She watched as Jada and Crystal laughed as if they were standing chit-chatting with Dave Chappelle. "Odd thing is the first time I laid eyes on this dude I was standing in a window. You don't think it's odd that you have been watching them as if you were a kid on punishment stuck in the house?" Brittan spoke with sarcasm. She and Kierra shared a laugh.

"I just want to know what he is really on. He is really starting to creep me out." Kierra said not taking her eyes off Bryson until her cell phone rang. She pulled her phone from her back pocket. She looked up nervously at Brittany and whispered, "This Mark from work."

Brittany eyes widened, "See what he wants!"

As long as Kierra took waiting to answer the phone it stopped ringing. They just stood there in amazement looking at each other as though they were in need of being rescued. Kierra got a chime letting her know she had left a voicemail. The chime caused them to slightly jump. Then her phone rang again. She finally answered, "Hello."

"Hey, Kiera. This is Mark from Check 'N Go. Do you have a minute?"

Kierra had a look and almost called him stupid, "Yeah, Mark, what's up?"

"I am just calling to let you know there has been a problem at the check cashing place and we will not be needing your services at the Ferguson location. I will be in touch as soon as we have something available." Mark paused.

"What happened?' Kierra waited to see what he was going to say. She was hoping she sounded nervous and not guilty.

"Where have you been? Are you up under a rock? The city is being destroyed after the police shooting." Mark was sounding as if were impersonating Gary with the tea from the Rickey Smiley Morning Show.

"Oh. I heard about that. I didn't know it was getting out of hand like that." Kierra knew it was an issue but she didn't know it was a major problem. Mark went on to tell her that the National Guard were on their way and the governor declared the area a state of emergency. Kierra had pretty much lied up until hearing about the National Guard. They hadn't turned on the television. They were busy watching the people that were outside near the money they had just confiscated from the heist they participated in over two hours ago.

Brittany watched as Bryson talked on his phone and gave Jada a hug. He dapped Crystal up as though she was a dude and headed to his car. Jada and Crystal watched as Bryson pulled off. When he was no longer in site Jada called Brittany's phone and told her to come on outside. Kierra followed Brittany out the door.

"What made him leave?" Brittany asked.

"He got a call from someone telling him how they looting all the stores in North County. They out there with liquor, toiletries, clothes, shoes, and lottery tickets. Hell, the streets being flooded with all kind of merchandise is how he put it." Jada spoke with slanted red eyes. "Let's get this stuff out my truck."

Each one of them grabbed a duffle bag and headed inside. Jada was the last one in. As soon as they shut there was a knock on the door. The girls looked at each other and didn't know what to do next. Jada moved and whispered, "Follow me." She led them to her bedroom, "Brittany, you go answer the door. We will stay in here."

Brittany walked out the room towards the front door. She tipped toed all the way up to the door. She looked out the peephole and couldn't see the person's face on the other side of the door. The darkness pretty much hid the individual's face. Brittany cut on the porch light. She was relieved. She opened the door and was taken back.

"Well, well, well. What do we have here?" Bryson said with a devilish smirk.

Brittany could believe her eyes. Bryson stood in the doorway of her home with his silver forty-five Ruger pointed at the back of Richard's head.

Richard didn't want to make a sudden move. At this point he was pissed. He had put Brittany in a different category and thrown her in another. Richard instantly became disgusted with himself. He couldn't believe he had walked right into his own demise. He never saw this coming. He would had never expected Brittany to be that type of person. Richard mugged Brittany with the eyes of death. He had no idea what she wanted but he was anxious to find out. All he could think about was curiosity killing the cat. He had survived the odds of a dirty game. Richard couldn't believe the innocence Brittany had portrayed had caught him up. He chuckled to himself. He knew that's how the game went. He was semi-retired. Richard had gone from being in too deep to one foot out the game with the other right behind it.

Jada could hear what she thought was Bryson's voice. She walked out to see what was going on. Jada knew that Brittany would have been the last person to let him in.

Bryson watched Jada as she entered the room, "So, I don't get no invite to this here little party." Bryson waved the Ruger in a circular motion, "I only came back because one of you broads have my lighter. When I saw Richie Rich I knew this had to be my lucky day. Jada, you know this the kingpin of this here city." Bryson had spoken with such excitement. He was acting as though President Barack Obama was in their presence, "The streets say this nigga has money all over this city. He buries his money in yards and builds walls to hide his money in and everything. He sort of like that dude Frank Lucas. He just doesn't give back. You know how dude was giving out those turkeys in that movie."

No one said a word. They all just stood and watched Bryson as he spoke about Richard. The only one in the room who was wearing a smile continued to talk, "I was standing out there with y'all tripping like this one of Richie Rich's old spots. I thought it was odd when y'all didn't invite me in. I was like it must be money in here." Bryson stopped talking to Jada and positioned himself where Richard could see his face, "Do y'all know you all have a real life American Gangster in you alls presence? Okay, so where's the money, homeboy?" Bryson felt proud of himself. Although he was from Memphis, he spent a lot of time in St. Louis. He would drive up to meet with Sean and Danitra to get his poison to take back to flood the streets of Memphis. Ever since Richard and Sean experienced their dealings with the law Bryson had fallen on hard times. Bryson embodied 50 Cent's get rich or die trying anthem. He was doing anything for a few dollars. Sean envied Richard so much that was all he ever talked about when he was around Bryson. Sean was Richard's protégée and Richard didn't even know it. Sean had filled Bryson up with so much stuff about Richard that Bryson felt as if he knew Richard personally.

Crystal and Kierra could barely hear. They knew the situation they could overhear was not good. They began to stuff the bags in Jada closet they were trying to be as quiet as possible. Once they had the bags in Jada's neat closet they start quietly taking the clothes off the hangers and throwing them on top of the bags. Kierra decided to call the police when she felt the clothes had camouflaged the bags of money just right.

Richard noticed that the wall he built was no longer there. He knew it was money there but he didn't know who had it. He had become filled with anger and confusion. Richard couldn't bring himself to defend himself. He was too focused on getting at Brittany. He watched as tears began to roll down her face. He didn't know how to even respond. Richard was trying to figure out did Bryson let them know that this was one of his old spots and it was a possibility that money could be inside the wall. He was so confused that all he could do was what he found himself doing a lot lately. He prayed.

The sudden hollow echo of knuckles tapping on the door startled them all. Bryson instructed them to be quiet. The tapping stopped for a minute but within a few minutes, it started back. They all just stood there.

"Police." The knockers yelled out.

Jada looked at everyone and walked to the door. Bryson freaked out on the inside but he stood nervously trying to figure out his next move. Bryson just figured he would shoot his way out of the situation. He was so pissed that he didn't have bullets any bullets in his gun. They were all standing just feet from the door. If the police took five steps forward, he would be right there in the room with all of them.

"Sorry for interrupting, but the head of your neighborhood watched committee contacted our department and then we had an anonymous call. The neighborhood watch caller informed us that there was something strange taking place over here and a tad bit much of traffic coming from this residence." This was said by the caramel complexion officer which was dressed in his entire uniform. His cap was pulled very close to his eyes. The officers were both appalled because no one even answered, "Who are the owners of this residence?" he continued.

"She and I." Jada pointed to herself and Brittany.

"Okay gentlemen, I am going to need you guys to step outside." The officer stated.

The other officer stood in silence. He kept his hand on the top of his gun the entire time. Jada and Brittany watched as Bryson led the way and Richard along with the officers followed behind. They were barely out the door before Richard hauled off and punched Bryson in the back of his head. Bryson fell instantly.

Richard turned around and dapped up the officer that was doing the majority of the talking. Richard was relieved when he saw his first cousin, Keith, enter the room. Keith was the first born of his mother's oldest sister. Richard realized that this evening was not going to go as he expected. He thought that he and Brittany were going to have a nice discussion about taking their relationship to the next level. He had been longing for her for some quite some time now. He thought that after the conversation was done, she was going to give him every bit of her love and he was going to do the same in return. He explained to his cousin, Keith, how Bryson had caught him sleeping. He held back the part about feeling as though he had been set up by Brittany.

Brittany was having her own internal war. She came to the conclusion that the money she and her brother had just found belong to Richard. She was trying to figure out how this was going to go down. She felt just as betrayed as Richard was just feeling. Brittany didn't understand why he hadn't mentioned to her that he was the previous owner of her new residence. On the other hand, she kind of understood why. Richard had seen the wall still intact so she wanted to know what would be his next move on finding out where his money was.

Keith asked Richard what he wanted to do. Bryson hadn't moved since he had been hit. Richard let him know he was not about to have the conversation in front of his partner. He told him to go ahead do what he needed to because no one there was about to press any charges. Richard even suggested for Keith to arrest him. That's not what he really wanted but the walk he was trying to take suggested that there should not be an eye for an eye. Not at that very moment anyway.

Teresa Seals

Chapter Sixteen

Crystal had fallen asleep. She was so high that she couldn't think straight. Sleep was the only way she could bring her high down. Kierra was waiting to hear that everything was okay. Kierra didn't want to speak because she didn't want anyone to enter the room they were hiding in at the moment. Kierra knew what Bryson was capable of and she didn't want to have him make another example. She began to doze off while she was waiting. She was fighting to keep her eyes open as she was guarding the money. She was wondering if Bryson was going to look for them. She figured he probably thought that she and Crystal had left right after he did. Jada eventually walked into the room to let them know how the situation had just panned out.

Kierra and Crystal were laying across Jada's Queen Size bed. Jada had a pet peeve about people laying on or sitting on her comforter. She always took it off so it wouldn't get dirty. She didn't come in complaining when she noticed her friends on her bed. Her life could have been over messing around with Bryson. The comforter became the least of her worries.

As Jada was giving Kierra and Crystal updates, Brittany was pleading her case, "Richard, I am so sorry. I called you over here to give you information about Bryson and he pulled this mess!" Brittany paused.

"What's the information?" Richard didn't care if she could feel the wrath of him being pissed or not.

Brittany could tell he was upset. She looked passed his anger. She began to tell him why she called him over, "One night in December, I was asleep. I heard a very strange noise. The noise was so strange it woke me up out of my sleep. I didn't know where the noise was coming from. I ran to check on my son. When I noticed he was okay, I went to look out the window to see if the sound I had heard had come from the outside. I noticed it did. I saw a girl outside keying my neighbor's car. My neighbor had been having this girl do damage to his car a lot lately. He and his wife were trying to figure out who it was that was causing all this damage. I went to grab my phone so I could take a picture of the girl. When I came back to the window Bryson was standing with the girl. It looked as though they were arguing. Bryson then shot and killed the girl and placed her in the trunk of my neighbor's car. When I got up that morning the car was gone. I believe my neighbor Danitra put Bryson up to killing this girl. I later found out that Danitra and Bryson are cousins. Knowing that they are cousins my instincts have been proven to be correct. I just didn't know that the damage she was causing would equate to death."

"Who was the girl, Brittany?" Richard asked.

Brittany placed her head down and didn't look up. She spoke so softly that she was whispering, "It was Leslie Collins."

Tears slowly ran down Richard's face. He had a bad feeling about the entire incident as Brittany was giving her account of the night in December. He couldn't handle the information Brittany had given him. Richard knew that even in their biggest argument Leslie still would reach out to him. She was not able to go days without speaking to him. No matter how many women Richard was involved with Leslie held a special place in his heart. Quiet as kept Brittany was coming close to a spot right next to where Leslie's special place was located. She was there when students in their third-grade class would make fun of how he read. Leslie took it upon herself to make sure he would no longer struggle with his reading. His problem was zoning out while reading. Leslie didn't know that but she encouraged him to read aloud with a whisper. She even told him to record himself at times. Leslie knew that most people were their own worse critic. She figured that once he heard himself reading he would want to and would work on his reading skills so that he could do much better. Although they didn't date much throughout school, they remained close friends. Leslie had given him his love a reading. He read just about everything from James Patterson to Teresa Seals.

Leslie had started sleeping with the enemy. Sean tried to stay off the radar with his odd jobs but his conquest to conquer all women put him in another category on the radar. Sean somehow managed to stay out of most federal cases that were shut down the drug empires. He had a hidden agenda for Leslie. The king of St. Louis was in love with her but he wanted that spot. What was another way could he triumph over him and reign that spot? Divide and conquer was his game plan and he figured infiltrating the only person he envied would get him where he wanted to be.

Richard wanted to be irate with Brittany. He knew it wasn't her fault. She barely knew anything about him. The only thing she had ever heard had come from her friend Crystal.

Richard had heard enough. He was coming up with his plan as Brittany talked. When Brittany spoke about a picture that she saw on Facebook with Danitra, her old neighbor, Richard became livid. It all began to make sense to him now. Brittany watched as he pulled his cell phone to send someone a text message.

Teresa Seals

Chapter Seventeen

Brandon's face was being displayed on every network that you could think of. He was describing the events of the tragedy that plagued his community along with several others. People became outraged with the fact that certain ethnicities were being killed by officials who signed up to protect and serve. The outcry started to bring several community activists out in an uproar. People could be found chanting, no justice, no peace, and hands up don't shoot. Every journalist was acting like vultures to get his version of the horrific event. In the beginning, he enjoyed the perks. He was being treated as though he was a celebrity. Things took a turn for the worse. Brandon became exhausted as he re-lived that moment each time someone asked him about what happened when he and Mitchell were together on that dreadful day. The incident even brought his mother, Pat, to town. She had no ulterior motives like most of the people who were coming out of the woodwork. Just about everyone Brandon had ever encountered was trying to get in touch with him. He wasn't sure of what they wanted because he didn't have anything to offer them. He figured they just wanted information out of the horse's mouth.

Brandon has contemplated suicide. It didn't take him long to act upon his thoughts. He decided to take an enormous amount of pain pills. His child's mother found him passed out in the bathroom and immediately called for medical assistance. He was placed on suicide watch at a local hospital. His mother just wanted to make sure her baby was okay. Despite their differences, she loved her son. She just had a selfish way of showing him.

Brittany had some time off due to her place of employment being burnt down to the ground. She would be there for her brother every chance she had. She was about to miss the grand opening of Kierra's youth enrichment program. Brittany sat next to her brother's hospital bed. She watched as he appeared to be at peace. She was watching as the liquid from the IV decreased. She buzzed for the nurse to come change it. The nurse responded quickly. Brandon was getting special treatment from all the nurses. It was as if he were a celebrity. He had entered several homes as the world watched, supported and grew angry about the death of Mitchell. To most people he was an overnight sensation. He was getting his fifteen minutes of fame. Brandon just wasn't riding the waves and getting a monetary value for his current celebrity status.

While Brittany was sitting beside Brandon as he slept she decided to write a blog about her brother. She didn't want to say it was her brother because she didn't want to appear bias.

WHO IS REALLY ON TRIAL?

Just last night, I was awakened by hearing the name Brandon Gates. As I lay listening to waiting to hear what was about to unfold, I couldn't believe what I was hearing. As the world is sitting back being the judge, jury, and executioner of all those involved, I feel the need to shed some light on the situation, in regards to Brandon Gates.

Now the media has reported Brandon as having a warrant for his arrest for a misdemeanor theft and filing a false police report in St. Louis City. This is very irrelevant and very distracting to the matter at hand. While reporting this, several media outlets failed to mention Brandon was a college student attending a technical college within the city. A simple misunderstanding led to his involvement with the law. His mother had sent him a care package which he didn't receive. A mail mix-up took place and the police were called to solve the mix-up. Brandon had in his possession two forms of identification when the police arrived. One was from the state and the other was from the college he attended. As the officer retrieved both pieces of identification, as he held both pieces of identification, he asked Brandon was he Brandon Gates. Brandon replied no to the facetious question. This incident has grown way out of proportion. I would like some clarification on why the witness is being scrutinized as though he is the one on trial.

The media and other individuals are poking holes in Brandon's account of the event that took place. Brandon Gates's character does not need to be destroyed, due to the fact that he witnessed an injustice and police brutality took place. His mother has raised him to be a respectable young man. Brandon is a son, a loving father, a little brother, an uncle, and a working man contributing to this society.

As the world watches a mother and father grieve, an eyewitness life has been turned upside down. Brandon has had enough courage to step up to the plate to ensure that Mitchell Crawford will receive the justice which is due to him. Before you make unkind comments, keep in mind that justice for all is the mission in this movement. Brandon is the witness and not the one who pulled the trigger.

When the cameras go away, Brandon still has to cope with what he saw take place on August 9, 2014. I pray that he and his immediate family are able to pick up the pieces. As I close, I would like to add......I can be the biggest criminal this side of creation in your eyes, yet that has nothing to do with what my eyes have witnessed........

Brittany reread her blog post and then uploaded it the site. This wasn't what she usually blogged about. Her blogs were strictly geared towards entertainment. She featured unground rappers and upcoming comedians. Brittany had a diverse following. She didn't know how receptive her audience would be about her latest topic. Today wasn't the day she was worried. She really didn't care about losing followers. Brittany's concerned was her younger brother. She wanted the people to know about the person she loved and how bad he was taking the tragedy himself.

Brittany wanted to be a part of Kierra's grand opening but her brother needs her more. Kierra had used her portion of her five hundred thousand to invest in designing a program that empowered teen girls. She was able to purchase an abandoned school with the help of her real estate mentor. The school building had only been vacant for eighteen months. There wasn't much damage. It only required minor repairs. Kierra and Dominique found a small time contractor to complete the minor repairs. The repairs were complete and her plans had been made. Three months later from their heist, she was about accomplish one of her many goals.

Kierra ribbon cutting ceremony was underway. She expected a higher pay off when they took the money the day all the chaos in Ferguson had taken place. They had recently counted the money on the site of the Check 'N Go and they were just shy of four million dollars. When they actually counted the money the night of the altercation of Bryson holding Richard and the girl's hostage, it was exactly two million dollars. Kierra knew that wasn't right. She figured that the Brinks guy and Mark had to have stolen the money prior to them getting there. She had no way of actually proving it. Kierra knew Mark had to be behind it. She connected the dots and realized that's why Brittany couldn't find any surveillance tapes in the equipment. Mark had already beat her to it.

Kierra looked at the time. She had set a time that she wanted to be at the event well before it started. She checked her watched and realized she had three hours until that time. Kierra texted Brittany to see how she and Brandon were doing. She smiled when Brittany replied with the three selfies of her and Brandon eating ice cream. Kierra then texts Jada to let her know the time she was leaving and Jada replied letting her know she would meet her there. Right as she was headed to shower Dominique called her. He had to let her know just how proud he was of her. He couldn't wait until he and his group would be performing regularly. He wanted to talk about all the plans and events they could do. Kierra had to remind him that she needed to get ready and Crystal was waiting to do her hair. There was going to be several city officials and those that were going to help with funding certain programs. She didn't want to be late and give the wrong impression. She was not about to show up on "CP" time. Dominique congratulated her one more time and ended the call.

Kierra entered the bathroom with such grace. She was acting as if she was the most fabulous person in the world entering a room of very important people. Kierra stepped over into the shower. The water was cleansing and refreshing she could just hug herself. She thought about how Jada and Crystal first brought up the plan to take the money from their job. She was so against it at first. She expected the police to be showing up and investigating. She figured that the reason they were not knocking on any doors was due to the fact nearly every business in that area had been burnt down to the ground. After several conversations with Dominique about her future plans and the money she needed, it wasn't long before she hopped on board with Jada and Crystal. She just needed to get Brittany to agree with them or at least take them seriously. Then when they decided to just do it they knew Brittany wouldn't have the guts to turn her back on them.

Kierra turned off the water and let the past go on down the drain. She began to focus on the future. She stepped out of the shower. As she began to dry off she saw her phone flashing. She immediately picked up and began to wonder what would Mark want now.

"Hello," Kierra waited on Mark to speak his peace.

144

"Kierra, this is Mark from Check 'N Go." He paused and Kierra became instantly irritated with that. She knew exactly who he was and where he was from. She had his name and number locked into her cell phone. He continued, "I just wanted to give you an update on what was taking place. Well, I was trying to get you and your team at another site but an investigation is underway. When the fire Marshall, the insurance adjuster, and Check 'N Go administration went to survey the damages there was no trace of where the money had burned. It sounds like to me that they believe it was an inside job. But, hold on, here's the kicker, there was no surveillance equipment. They thought that could at least find and salvage the surveillance equipment. It didn't happen. The only other place with cameras that they could have used would be the QT surveillance equipment and that was burned down to the ground just like our equipment." Mark ended his statement as if he were quite happy.

Kierra thanked him for updating her. She told him to contact her if he found out anything new or need her to help with anything. Kierra wanted to ask him so bad about the money missing but his demeanor through the phone confirmed the feeling. She always thought that Mark and the white man from the Brinks were too chummy. Kierra was lost in her thoughts. She started thinking about the trouble she and her friends could have been in had they not did what they had did. Being that all the money was not there, either her shift or the second shift may have seemed as though they were the culprits. Kierra ran to Crystal's room. She had to get her hair touched up and let her know what happened when Mark had called.

"What the fuck?!" Kierra couldn't believe her eyes. She almost lost it. When she noticed that Crystal was unresponsive she knew she had to regain her composure. She stopped, took a deep breath, and called out for Crystal's mom. She didn't get an answer. Kierra realized she had her cellphone in her hand and began to dial 911.

145

She spoke with the dispatcher and was informed that the medical officials were on their way. Kierra dialed Jada next. She didn't give Jada time to say hello. She cut her off in mid hello, "Jada what are you doing?"

"I am getting ready so I can be at your ribbon cutting ceremony on time. I am trying to put together something so fly that when people see these photos that they forget all about the Diamonds in the Ruff and focus on my outfit. Why are you calling me anyway? We just talked." The excitement Jada had about her outfit wasn't important to Kierra at all.

Kierra took a deep breath, "I am standing over Crystal and I just checked her neck and her wrist for her pulse. Her pulse is there but it is real weak," tears began to quickly roll down Kierra's face.

Jada paused. She grew in frustration from her confusion, "Say what now? Is her pulse weak? What the hell is she doing?"

Kierra just stood there frozen, "She looks dead but there is a needle on the floor and this belt is tied around her arm." Kierra began to breathe harder as the tears immensely emerged.

"I am on my way." Jada didn't even hang up. She just held the phone, grabbed her keys and was out the door.

Jada made it to the house before the ambulance. When she pulled up Crystal's mom was walking in the front door. Jada pushed past her and ran to Crystal's room. The ambulance pulled up and began to approach the house. Crystal's mom went after Jada. The EMT workers didn't know what to do. They stood there for a minute trying to figure out what their next move was going to be. They checked to make sure they had the right address. A screeching sound came from the house they were standing in front of, they decided to follow the screams. When they approached Crystal's room, they knew they were in the right place.

Teresa Seals

Chapter Eighteen

Richard sat in his uncle's old blue beat up pickup truck. He could see out but no one could see in. He had been watching Sean's front door for the last three days. No one had come in or went out the door the entire time he was sitting there watching the door. The first day wasn't that easy for him to just sit on the block and go unnoticed. There were so many people just hanging out he had to rectify the situation. He contacted his cousin and asked him did he still have any friends that worked in the city for St. Louis Metropolitan Police Department. When Keith confirmed he knew someone Richard let him know what he needed him to do for him. Keith had called one of his friends that were a hothead when he first joined the police force.

Within thirty minutes, the police had swarmed the block and cleared off the street. They rolled through the block every ten minutes until no one was no longer outside. It had been three months since Mitchell's death caused such an uproar. There was so much tension with the citizens and the police at the time. No one wanted to be the next victim of police brutality. People still could be found throughout the city protesting. They were not just out there protesting for Mitchell because there were three more young men who had been brutally murdered by the police. They were protesting against police brutality. Black Lives Matter became known as the new civil rights movement. The phrase was coined after a young black was killed in Florida.

The movement went from a protest cry to a political force. The protesters wanted the world to know that black lives matter because they were they only lives in jeopardy being taking by the hands of police. The people that populated the street gave up and found another hangout spot. They were not doing anything constructive they were just hanging out socializing. The destruction was taking place the next block over. The officers cleared that block out too for the time being as well. Half of the people that hung out on either of the two blocks were not from the neighborhood anyway.

Richard didn't worry about anyone calling in reporting a strange vehicle. Sean and Danitra didn't live in that type of area. The only one who may have recognized it and would have called it in would've been Mrs. Harris. She was no longer amongst the living. Richard literally had no worries. Derelict cars were all over this area and they would go ignored. Someone would assume that it was just broken down. If abandon car sat too long, it became the neighborhood chair. Any and everybody would sit on it and that would be the spot everyone would just be hanging out around. The little kids of the neighborhood would make any abandoned car their playground until some adult would tell them to get off the vehicle. If the owner wanted the property, they would retrieve it or it would eventually be towed by St. Louis city. Richard knew he was fine as he sat and watched everything that was moving. He only pulled off to relieve his bladder, intestines, and grab a bite to eat. He only left the block when no one was outdoors. He tried to limit his time off the block. Richard didn't want to miss his moment of opportunity.

The October weather was feeling more like winter night's chill so he would occasionally start the car to knock off the little chill the would sporadically visit the truck. On the night Richard thought was his last, he texts his cousin, Keith, to tell him to let Bryson go and he would take care of it. He had already premeditated how he was going to seek the revenge for Leslie's death.

Richard sat there thinking about how goofy Leslie was but yet so smart. He looked over at Nina and the books which were sitting next to him. His bible and a book he was reading. Richard grabbed his bible and placed it under his seat and picked up the other book he had sitting on the seat. He was reading Alfred Powell's Message *'N a Bottle: The 40oz Scandal*. Richard was finding this book to be a bit fascinating with a conspiracy twist. It made him think about things that are targeted toward the African-American population to destroy them or keep them stagnant. He even conducted a self-evaluation while he was reading the book. He thought about how he contributed to the destruction of the African-American population as he once flooded the city with his poison. As we were about to pick up the book and get back to it, he was distracted. He watched as a car slowed down as if it were checking him out but the individual parked on the opposite side of the street, two cars up. As soon as he saw the dreads his heart started to beat increased. When he looked to see the individual who had come out to greet Bryson is heartbeat intensified. He could feel his adrenaline as it was increasing.

Richard thought about the sole reason him and Sean paths crossed in the first place. It made him think about their very first encounter.

Everyone knew that Richard had the city on lock. When he was in the game he had organized crime down to a science. No one but his friends he had first started hustling with knew what he looked like. Other than that most didn't have a face to match the name that was ringing bells. Richard was humble as they come. His major mistake came when he started hanging in the circle with other name ringers.

One summer night he walked into the Tap Room. The Tap Room was a hole in the wall lounge not far from where he grew up. He entered wearing a white tee and Levi's with fresh white Nikes. The rose gold Presidential Rolex and the way he walked demanded respect. The watch and the walk let the onlookers know he was somebody.

150

Everybody was checking for him. He went back and sat with Rico "Squeaky" Petty. He had gotten the name Squeaky from his high pitched voice. It was not as high pitched as Michel'le. It was just too high for a male.

Squeaky was the reason he was out. He had asked him to stop by and have a drink with him. Squeaky was the oldest player known in the city. Squeaky was hot during the time Run DMC was kicking down doors and telling folks how their Adidas were cold on their feet with no shoestrings in them. Squeaky was the Michael Jordan of the dope game in St. Louis in his prime. Squeaky had retired and went out the game like Kobe. Some wanted him to leave and others hated to see him go. He had his hand in all kinds of business ventures. He owned three liquor stores, two laundromats, three gas stations, and a strip mall parking lot. Squeaky had pull with police and the politicians. No one knew his secret to success and remaining to be free. They were trying to find out. Squeaky saw something in Richard when he met him and took him under his wing. The minute Richard was arrested Squeaky disassociated himself. The cut-off was similar to the way Paulie did Henry Hill in Goodfellas.

Richard was on his way out the Tap Room and was headed to his car. Some scrambling jack boys were coming for his Rolex. They were in the lounge and purposely left out to wait on Richard to leave. He was an unknown individual to them. Being that he was unknown meant that he was fair game. They would take his belongings but let him keep his life.

Sean just so happen to intervene. Sean left out the Tap Room with perfect timing. Sean personally knew the jack boys. They were d-boys from his hood. He knew that entire situation was not going to end well with them. Squeaky would have seen to it himself. Sean walked over as Richard was about to take off his watch. Richard was boiling hot. He couldn't believe he walked into the Tap Room without his burner. It was in the secret compartment in his BMW. Richard knew he would be amongst a bunch of stand-up dudes and it wasn't any real need for his gun so he thought. He didn't expect to leave out alone. Richard figured others would have left when he did. He knew these young cats were making a grave mistake. He wasn't even trying to warn these goofy dudes.

Sean walked right up, "Y'all don't even realize the danger you all are in. Did you all not see him breaking bread with Squeaky? This the wrong dude to be trying to jump off the porch on. So, y'all go ahead and get out of here why y'all can."

Just like that, they were gone. Sean was a respected individual at the time. For a minute, Richard thought it was a setup. At that moment he didn't care. He was pissed at himself. Richard couldn't believe that he got himself in that type of predicament. He thanked Sean for looking out for him. He vowed never to let anyone catch him like that again. The entire time he was in the game he never left his house without Nina. He and Sean dapped it up but Sean was a man with a purpose and Richard would soon find out.

Sean had been sending Danitra to Texas to pick up his work ever since she was fourteen. The trips were easy for the hustling couple. Danitra would catch a flight to meet the drug connect, Joe. Joe was originally from St. Louis. He relocated to Texas to be closer to the Mexican border. She would come back from Houston with six to eight bricks taped to her small frame. Like most drug mules they had the smoothest smuggling taking place. All that changed when the collapse of the World Trade Center took place. Sean had to find him a new connect. Danitra and Sean lavish lifestyle became just a lifestyle. The money was not coming in like it once was. Sean was hurting. He had a job as a janitor along with other side hustles. It just wasn't the same as having money on top of money. Sean needed more than his paycheck. That's why he was off in the game in the first place. His job was just the front.

The next time Richard saw Sean was at Squeaky's fiftieth birthday party. Danitra was with Sean and Leslie was with Richard. After a few encounters, Danitra and Leslie became close associates. They would hang out on occasions. Sean had finessed Danitra to where she was cool with Sean working on Leslie. Leslie would be the pawn that was going to help him get to Richard's connect. Sean became a co-defendant. Sean was making sure he remained a free man and Richard happened to be connected to the same case. Sean was not telling on Richard. He was telling on someone Richard was connected to. Richard went to jail and Leslie fell in love with Sean. She wasn't trying to but it just happened. Leslie had played her side-chic role for just about nine years. She wanted him to leave Danitra but he wasn't going for it. Leslie was tired of keeping quiet. Richard had gone to jail and while he was there he found out about her relationship. She wasn't looking back. When she lost her place because Richard stopped paying the mortgage, she wanted Sean to step up to the plate. Leslie felt that it was Sean's fault in the first place.

Leslie began to threaten his freedom all while she was causing havoc and chaos in his life. Sean had to get rid of his problem and Danitra's cousin Bryson would help him.

Richard eased up on Sean and Bryson. They were arguing about the money Sean owned Bryson. When Richard approached the two of them, they were experiencing the scariest day of their life. They realized that Richard was seeking his revenge for Leslie as he stood there with them with Nina in his hand.

"Dude, I saved your life that night. That don't mean anything?" Sean looked as if he saw a ghost. He was referring to the first encounter he and Richard had.

"Yea, but you took the only thing I cared about." Richard had to rebuttal and hold back his tears just thinking about the love of his life.

Bryson was about to grab his burner from his waist. Richard placed Nina to Bryson's temple, "I will push your shit back right here!"

Richard didn't want to contribute to black on black crime. He contemplated but he knew dead men didn't talk back. Richard waved Nina in their face as he instructed them to walk in the house. This scene was about to play out like a movie. Richard let Sean know he may as well lead him to the safe.

Richard wanted to call him a snitching ass nigga but he refrained from saying too much. There was no need to. He was impressed with the front Sean and Danitra had. Sean worked a nine to five. His handy skills were a front to deliver his work. Richard laughed when Brittany told him Danitra was waiting to get a disability check. She had never worked an honest job in her life.

Teresa Seals

Chapter Nineteen

Brittany was responding to the comments her followers were posting on her blog. She hadn't been blogging as much as she used to. However, when she added anything the followers flocked to it. She had called Kierra to see how Crystal was doing. After finding out that her friend was up laughing and talking she was relieved. Brittany was glad to hear that even under the circumstances Kierra didn't miss her ribbon cutting ceremony. Diamonds in the Ruff was about to get exposure on Brittany's blog. She was even thinking about creating a go fund me account to link to the commentary. She knew that Kierra needed all the donations she could get. They were being so discreet with their recent riches they had stumbled upon the extra funds could help cover up any frivolous spending.

Brittany called to check on her son. Jarvis, Jr. was having so much fun with his grandparents he didn't want to come home. He had even started going to school from his grandparents' house. Brittany hadn't planned on him moving in but it just happened. No one even spoke about the arrangements. Janice, Jarvis's mom, told Brittany she wanted him to attend Cleveland Preparatory Academy. It was a prestigious school that received the National Blue Ribbon every year. The ribbon represented the schools that have achieved high levels of performance and made significant improvements in closing the achievement gap.

Jarvis days of daycare in the morning and evening had come to an end. Hanging around his mom and her friends had also come to an end. When he was with Brittany his weekends consisted of Chuck E. Cheese, going out to eat and shopping at various malls. His grandparents were exposing him to something else other than shopping. He had seen what the city of St. Louis had to offer. Jarvis had been to the Gateway Arch, The Dred Scott Museum, The Butterfly House, and The Griot Museum of Black History. Jarvis had even crossed the bridge to check out the Cahokia Mounds. The remnants of the most sophisticated primitive native evolution north of Mexico were located there. They had eaten at nearly all the restaurants which were considered fine dining. His mother and her friends exposed him to restaurants but it was not the same thing. He had enough of Apple Bees and Red Lobster. He was eating caviar from Franco's, oysters from Broadway Oyster Bar, steaks from Ruth Chris, and lobster from Gulf Shores. They had plans to go out of town but they felt it was important to be aware of what where he lived had to offer.

Jarvis grandparents told him they were going to expose and introduce him to things he wouldn't know existed. They wanted him aware, inquiring, reading and thinking. Jarvis was going to be successful if they had anything to do with it. He had been spending so much time with Jarvis's parents he didn't even get to see Brittany's mother when she was there for two days visiting Brandon.

When Jarvis's mother answered the phone she greeted her and asked her had she talked to Jarvis lately. His mother let her know she spoke with him that morning. Brittany instantly got very emotional. He hadn't called her. As soon as she hung up the phone, Jarvis walked through the door. She was at a loss for words. Jarvis just smiled. He stood there looking like Idris Elba and possessing his T.I. swag. Brittany hopped up and ran to the toilet. She was throwing up and she figured it was from the nervousness she was experiencing. She didn't even know what to say. Brittany cleaned her face and went over to hug him. She didn't want to let go.

Jarvis released her and turned her around. He pointed to the television in the hospital room, "Isn't that over there where you use to live?"

The news was reporting a triple homicide. As the reporter stood in front of Sean and Danitra's house, Brittany watched in bewilderment. The reporter stated the police department was investigating but at the moment there were not any leads on the suspects. Brittany knew exactly who the suspect was. She knew who killed them and she knew why they had been killed. There was a greater possibility that she knew who the third victim was. She didn't believe that Richard was even capable of such a heinous crime. When he was giving her the backdrop of his life he never made mention of him being a murderer. She knew he wouldn't just act as though she were a Catholic Priest and confessed all of his sins to her.

Brittany was thinking realistically about his street status and the respect he painted of himself as he told her how he once was on top of the world. The entire time he was speaking she thought of movies such as *Scarface*, *The Godfather*, and *Goodfellas*. Neither one of those gangster movies were free from killings. She knew that it wasn't any way he could have walked away from the game without any blood on his hands. Brittany knew he was very capable of a triple homicide.

Brittany had Richard heavy on her mind. She would look over at Brandon and pray he would wake up. Brandon was doing much better. No one had to tell Brittany that her brother was suffering from depression. Brittany knew he was just trying to sleep away his problems. For a short time, he was suffering from sleep deprivation. The first few months after Mitchell was murdered he was afraid to go to sleep. He said every time he closed his eyes he relived that horrible moment.

She was very uncomfortable sitting there with Jarvis. Brittany wanted to call Jada but she knew she would ask a thousand questions. She looked at her phone it was so much she wanted to do with that phone, but she couldn't. Brittany knew she could not just text anyone without them calling to inquire and if she did text it would not have been just one or two text messages. Anyone she would have called would have wanted to have a conversation be it on the phone or through text message. This day was not as she expected. Brittany and Jarvis had spoken so many times about what they would do once he was a free man. They just didn't talk about him not warning her or at least informing her of this day. Brittany was at a different place in her life. She had Richard heavy on her mind. She needed to talk to him. Brittany wanted to know how he was doing. The changed man she was falling for had just did what she considered to the unthinkable. Brittany stopped thinking about Richard and focused on Jada.

Brittany and Jada had only had the conversation about their living arrangements when they first purchased the house together. Jada agreed that she would move out by the time Jarvis was due to be released. She wanted to live in the downtown area in a loft so that's where she was going when the time presented itself. Since their financial situation had changed Jada was focused on getting *Pink Legacy Boutique* established. Brittany knew moving out so that she and Jarvis could be a family was nowhere in Jada's plan at that moment. Brittany realized that Jarvis was a big inconvenience. She noticed he was looking and staring at her. She wasn't ready to speak about anything. Jarvis figured that Brittany was thinking about the death of her neighbors. Little did he know that Sean and Danitra were not anywhere on her mind. Her thoughts were circled around him not fitting in the equation of Jada and Richard.

Brittany called Demeasha to find out how she and the baby were doing. Demeasha hadn't been up to the hospital after she and Pat had a big blow up. Brandon had shared with Demeasha that his mother hadn't spoken to him since she had left for Arizona the day after Brittany had graduated. Demeasha was trying to keep the peace up until Pat started to try to run things. Pat was dishing out orders to the hospital staff and the moment she told Demeasha that her baby shouldn't be up there things took a turn for the worse.

"Mrs. Gates, you don't know me but I do know that you are a woman who didn't acknowledge the father of your children. Whatever reason you chose to keep the man out of their lives was your business. I am not you and you are not me. As long as Brandon is in our lives we are going to be by his side. Did it ever dawn on you that you are part of the reason he's lying here in this hospital bed recouping from trying to end his life?" Demeasha didn't get loud. She was very stern. She spoke very calmly. She looked Pat directly in her eyes. Brittany stood next to Demeasha in solidarity. Pat grab her purse and did what she did best. She turned her back on her kids once more.

Demeasha apologized to Brittany but she let her know that Brandon struggled with his past. She didn't go into details on the countless days of Brandon spent pouring his heart out about his mother. Although he was to blame for the majority of it. He let Demeasha know his life had never been the same since his grandmother took her last breath. Brittany just listened to her. She didn't know what to say. Brittany lost her mother for a minute but she had her aunt. Along with having her aunt, she had Jada, Crystal, and Kierra. Her friends were her family.

Brittany was full of resentment Brandon for what he had done but she still loved him. She didn't grow close to him when they were in foster care because she was mad about what he had done. Brittany had given him the cold shoulder at times. That's why she was sitting there now in the hospital room. She never wanted Brandon to feel as though he didn't have any family. Brittany held turned her back on him once, she was not about to do it again.

Demeasha let Brittany know that when her mother came to get the baby she would be back up there. Brittany ended the call. She looked over at Jarvis and asked him what he wanted to do. He let her know he was content just being there with her. Brittany wasn't feeling

160

his affection. She wanted him to leave so that she could contact Richard and see how he was doing. Brittany thought about just leaving and going outside to call him but she knew in her heart that Jarvis would just follow her outside. She leaned back in the chair and closed her eyes to rest.

Brittany opened her eyes when she heard a few usual voices. They were laughing and catching up on old times. Brandon was up talking with Jarvis, Jada, Kierra and Crystal. Brittany was glad to see Crystal. She didn't look like anything she had been through. Her girls let her know they had to come check on her and Brandon. They informed her that her phone was going straight to voicemail. Brittany turned it off before she fell asleep. She didn't want Richard's face to come across the screen when and if he called.

Kierra let her know that she had planned a road trip. They were going to Atlanta, Georgia. She had an entire itinerary of what they were going to do when they got there. Jada put everything and everyone at ease. She let Jarvis know he would be rooming with them for the time being. Jada let them all know that she wasn't leaving until she had gotten herself established. She had to let them know money wasn't the issue, she just didn't want to add too much to her plate. She was going to focus on one thing at a time. Brittany listened to Kierra's plans and Jada's details were interpreted at the moment that nothing or no one from the past would dictate her future.

Kierra, Crystal, and Brittany knew that money wasn't the issue. Kierra had let them know that they needed to be careful with their spending. The corporate office of Check 'N Go had contacted her when she began to make headlines with her Diamond in the Ruff organization. The company wanted to be recognized as a sponsor. Kierra had a low-key joke because they were the ones who sponsored and helped out with establishing the program in the beginning. Kierra was a little leery of the attention but she was not worried. Mark, their supervisor from Check 'N Go had brought attention to himself as he and his wife began to take extravagant trips. He was under investigation from the time he posted him and wife pictures on social media. Kierra instructed them to be smart about the moves they made.

Chapter Twenty

Jada was about to exit Interstate 285 to head towards the Hyatt Regency in downtown Atlanta. She headed towards Greenville/Augusta and took exit 29 to Ashford-Dunwoody Road. Kierra started off driving. She drove four two hours and then Crystal drove for the next two hours. The last two hours were divided up between Brittany and Jada. Jada pulled into the hotel's parking lot with time to spare. Kierra had stayed awake with Jada while the other two slept. When the car came to a halt Brittany woke up. She tweeted to her followers that she was in the ATL. By the time they entered the hotel to check in Brittany received a direct message on Twitter. One of the rappers, Young Sic, had let her know that The Rickey Smiley Morning Show was having a charity event and she should come out to support since she was in town. He went on to inform her that other local celebrities would be in attendance. He went on further to tell here that the coverage she could obtain would make a nice blog topic. After reading the long message, Brittany replied to the message to find out the location of the event. Young Sic asked her location. When she told him she was downtown he let her know the Atlanta Comedy Theater was about thirty minutes from where she was. He then gave her the address and told her he would see her there.

Brittany let Kierra know that she needed to add the charity event to her itinerary. Jada needed to know what celebrities were going to be there.

"Okay, I know we are in Hotlanta and my chances of seeing Fiddy and becoming a millionaire is slim to none. However, I can give Tiny a run for her money and have Tip taking me to Lennox Mall. I'll have him up in the joint telling me I can have whatever I like!" Jada laughed. Kierra looked at her friends and they all shared a laughed. They checked in and headed towards their room. Kierra had reserved one room with double beds. Even with the money, they had stashed in safes that were hidden in their homes, they still didn't do things beyond their means.

The Rickey Smiley and Friends Benefit show started in two hours. Crystal touched up everyone's hair. There wasn't much she had to do for Jada. She had recently done her braids. Kierra and Brittany both had added Brazilian weave to their hair. They were looking like Kerry Washington's *Scandal* character by the hair. Crystal tightening up both their curls. The curls would eventually be loose and fall perfectly.

Brittany pulled out the light green chiffon dress with the diamond brooch that Jada had made for her. The slit in the front of the dress exposed her breast and portion of her stomach area. Brittany didn't care about the slight chill from Atlanta's November weather. Brittany had left her conservativeness in St. Louis. She was feeling like Beyoncé's alter ego Sasha, flawless and fierce. Brittany had Jada take a picture of her. She sent it to Richard. Jada pulled out her pink chiffon dress it was short and tight. Jada's dress didn't expose as much skin as the dress she made for Brittany but they were about the same length.

Kierra wore an all-white pantsuit. The white blazer made it very obvious that she didn't have on a bra as a portion of her stomach area was exposed but it fit her nicely. Crystal had opted for some True Religion skinny jeans with an all-black long Versace thermal like shirt and black Victoria Christian Louboutin. The shoes were the most expensive item Crystal had spent her money on.

The girls were on their way to see Rickey Smiley. When they reached their destination they realized that Young Sic failed to mention that the need to purchase tickets to even attend the event. As they were about to leave due to the fact they couldn't get into the sold out show, the Queen of Atlanta was coming through the door. Jada was the first to recognize the bite size little woman. Jada was so excited to see Ms. Juicy. She was so impressed that Jada was a fan, she led them backstage. Their attire led Ms. Juicy to believe they were somebody. As the four girls were about to pass by her she reacted to the fact the girls smelled like money.

When they were on their way to Juicy's dressing room they bumped into Rickey Smiley in the hallway. Mr. Smiley was looking casket sharp in his all-white. His swag was everything. Rickey embodied Murphy Lee's *Not A Stain* as he rocked his outfit and his personal frames from America's Best Contacts and Eyeglasses. He was so humble. The girls were impressed with how down to earth he was. Kierra let him know about her foundation and he agreed to come out and help support her in her endeavors. Kierra dropped him a stack and told him that was for his foundation. Jada, Crystal, and Brittany looked at Kierra as if she were crazy. The thousand dollars she had just blessed The Rickey Smiley Foundation with was from Check 'N Go heist.

Rickey handed the money off to a guy he said worked for him. He turned to Kierra, "Dang! Are you doing it like that? I know where I'm going when this show is over. I can introduce you to my monkey stomp!" Rickey joked. He gave them all a hug and walked off to start his show. The girls were able to watch the show for free on the side of the stage.

As the comedy show was taking place, Brittany was tweeting and hashtagging. She was also putting notes on her cell phone. Brittany was going to make her next blog about the event. Brittany thought about Jarvis and their living arrangements. He had been living with her and Jada since his release. Jarvis had just been hanging around. He couldn't find work so he enrolled into a program that helped convicted felons in their job search. Things begin to look up for him. She didn't want to be the person who was known as the hope killer but this trip she was on made her realized Jarvis was a part of her past. Brittany wanted Jarvis to know that they could be friends but she wanted the relationship part of it to remain in her past. She was ready to take it to the next level with Richard. Brittany wanted to remain friends with Jarvis. She wanted to be friends on the strength of her son. For a brief moment, she began to think of how she should have done things differently with Jarvis in the beginning. There was trying times but she sustained. Her feelings were unconditional in the beginning. Her love had changed. She thought Jarvis was meant for her. Brittany heard laughter and it snapped her out of her thoughts.

The comedy show was over and Kierra suggested that they head over to Club Onyx. When they made it to the club they could see the black and gold sign with Onyx on it. They parked and headed inside. It was not what Kierra expected. Kierra looked at Jada and Jada looked back at her. Brittany was looking like she was ready to go. Crystal walked in and led the way. Everyone was hesitant to follow but when it seemed as though Crystal was not about to leave, they went on ahead and followed her. Fetty Wap's *Trap Queen* was the DJ's music choice. The club went wild. The strippers were doing all sorts of handstands and twerk-off competitions. Brittany smiled listening to the *Trap Queen* lyrics. Brittany then text Richard.... *Hi! Just thinking about you!*

Jada stood at a stand-still tapping her friend on her shoulder. Brittany looked up from her phone. Brittany looked at Jada to see what she wanted. Jada hadn't said a word or even looked at Brittany. She just followed Jada's eyes. Jada had spotted her second celebrity.

"I just want to run over there and take his picture. I just don't want to appear as if I'm a groupie." Jada leaned over and yelled in Brittany's ear. She was trying to make sure Brittany heard her over the music. Jada watched Jeezy until she no longer seen him in her view. Everyone else in the club acted as though he was an average Joe.

Watching the other individuals react to his presence caused her to do the same. She refrained from pulling her phone out and snapping a picture. Crystal and Kierra were standing in the same vicinity for a second. Then they walked away. Crystal was moving and grooving. She was having a good time. She was the best dancer of the four of them

It was three in the morning when the club closed. Jada was the only one that was amped up as they left Club Onyx. As they were leaving out the door she laid eyes on Jeezy and Lil Boosie. The two rap stars together put her energy on ten. Jada got the opportunity to take a picture with the both of them. The entire conversation was about that picture and how she was about to move to Atlanta. Everyone else could barely keep their eyes open. They made it safely back to the Hyatt and called it a night.

They had slept well unto the afternoon. Brittany got up to check her phone. There was no message from Richard but Jarvis had sent a message.

Good morning, love.
Call me when you have some downtime.

Brittany read it and ignored it. She thought to herself, "You may not want to hear what I have to say. You go ahead and wait for that call."

Brittany pulled out her MacBook. She began her write up on the charity event she and her girls had attended. The entire time Brittany was creating the blog, she couldn't stop laughing. She laughed so hard that she woke Kierra up.

Kierra looked around, "What time is it? Why you let us sleep this long? We are going to the World of Coca-Cola and the Georgia Aquarium today."

Brittany looked at Crystal and Kierra. They were in a deep sleep. Brittany leaned her head in their sleeping direction, "You need to wake them up, don't you?"

Kierra turned the television on. She flipped through the channels. She stopped when she saw Queen Latifah's face on the television screen. She looked at Brittany. Brittany looked back at her. Brittany's face told Kierra, "Don't even say a word." Kierra laughed.

Kierra ignored what Brittany's face was saying, "Just think if this movie ended differently. What if they all just got away?"

Brittany actually thought that Kierra was going to suggest that they started robbing banks. When she realized it was just a normal conversation she could take part in, she replied, "I always said, if T.T. hadn't listened to Cleo they would have probably got away. But, it's a movie that's how the person planned it out. That's to tell people like Jada and Crystal making decisions like that don't always end well. I couldn't even imagine my life without you girls. Every time I would hear Brandy say *though I'm missing you*, damn, I wouldn't find a way to get through or get by. You all are my sisters." Brittany instantly became saddened just by saying the beginning lyrics. She grew empty inside and couldn't hide her tears.

Kierra understood. Brittany's statement was mutual and heartfelt. She sat right next to Brittany on the bed. Kierra whispered, "I have been thinking about how we could get more money. I have been trying to figure away. The first time was so smooth. It's a good thing we haven't run through that money so there hasn't been a rush to get some more money. I was thinking once they are done rebuilding Check 'N Go how we could get some more money."

Brittany couldn't believe what she was hearing. She always looked at Kierra and thought she was the smartest one out of the group. She was feeling very differently. Brittany found the words to say and just hoped they came out right. She took a deep breath, "Kierra, baby wake up. We did it one time and got away with it. We are not living on a movie screen. That went so well for us. Have you ever thought about had the whole entire situation wouldn't happen the way it did, that we might be in jail anyway? Did you forget Mark stole the money first? We almost could have got caught for something we hadn't done. Besides, if we not pulling stunts like they did in *Takers*, I'm not put myself in that situation again. Ask me about committing another robbery when one of y'all learn how to fly a helicopter."

Jada woke up, "Everybody knows, almost doesn't count?"

Brittany stood up, "We can end this conversation! We got away with it and being greedy trying to go for seconds will not end well. You better use the money you already have and find a way to invest in you. I swear I will walk away from all of you and won't look back. I am not going to jail. My freedom is not about to be jeopardized. I already feel like I have abandon my son, but I have the opportunity to go to see him anytime I feel like it. I can't do that from no jail cell."

Kierra stood up to head to the bathroom, "Girl, you sound like T. T. What about my son?" Kierra whined as though she was one of the characters from *Set It Off*. "It was just a thought. We will all reap the benefits for the Diamonds in the Ruff organization." Kierra had majored plans for her not-for-profit organization.

Brittany headed to the bathroom to take her shower. She was upset that she didn't get a chance to finish her blog. She figured she would get done while everyone else was getting ready. Brittany wanted to reply to Jada's almost doesn't count comment. She wanted to let her know how she felt so bad. Brittany wanted to throw up in Jada's face that she could not even stand the rain when she's was in a storm. She was referring to how Jada didn't visit her grandparents often. Her mother was back and she was avoiding her at all cost. So she knew you couldn't take the pressure from the authorities had they began to be investigated. Jada would eventually talk. She would not have been able to fight the urge of telling how smooth they had done what they had done.

They were ready and headed out the door within two hours. Brittany had typed, edited and uploaded her blog. While they were at the World of Coca-Cola Brittany looked to see how much traffic her blog received since she had posted. She had more traffic than she ever had before. Rickey Smiley had added it to his foundation website and the morning show website. Brittany was feeling famous like Kim K for a brief second. As they were leaving the museum Brittany wanted to get her son a souvenir. When they made their exit and headed over to the Georgia Aquarium the lady that had taken their tickets was named Beverly. Beverly was heavy on their mind because the guide at Coca-Cola told them to be sure to try the Beverly. The Beverly was an Italian beverage which was very bitter. Beverly let them know that drink was discontinued but the museum still has it as a sample. She continued telling them that she had the same conversation will nearly everyone that left the museum and came over to the aquarium.

They were done with two things Kierra had on her list to do. Crystal let them know that she needed to get some rest. She couldn't do another thing or visit another attraction. She had sampled too many coke products for one. She was having a sugar rush. Crystal hadn't had any sort of drugs since her overdose scare. She didn't have the energy she once had and she couldn't explain it. Crystal went to sleep often to fight the drug urges. She was making the adjustment from not doing or using the excessive amount drug use she had partaken in. Kierra was watching her like a hawk. She was trying to remember if they were any possibilities had she gotten a hold to anything while they were at Club Onyx. Kierra agreed with Crystal and headed back to the hotel. She along with everyone else needed to rest up before they got on the road.

Brittany had checked her phone the entire day. She had not received the one call from the one person she was looking to call her. Jarvis called her and she couldn't help but let him know what the plan was for their future. Jarvis agreed. He let her know he could sense that. Jarvis wasn't upset and he let her know that. He was surprised to see that the relationship they had lasted that long. He let her know if it was meant to be they will be able to work that out. Jarvis wanted to elaborate more but he didn't. He noticed that he hadn't seen her smile since his arrival. The night they were intimate he could feel the disconnect. He was still in love with her. He just blamed it on the time apart. Brittany was his first true love. He was going to right the wrongs. Brittany was going to love him like she once did. He was going to be the man for her. Jarvis let Brittany know he would be at his parents when she made it back.

Jada had overheard Brittany's and Jarvis's conversation. Apart from her didn't feel comfortable leaving him in the house with the money. The other part of Jada felt it was safe. It was in the attic at the far end. Her portion was locked in one safe and Brittany's portion was in the other safe. The two steal fireproof safes were sitting side by side. There was no direct view of the safe so she felt they were safe from being seen. The attic was a small crawl space storing a few boxes. The installation gave the attic an awkward smell. It was very creepy so she didn't see anyone just going up there just to be hanging out. She put the thought out of her mind. She needed to enjoy the time she had left in Atlanta. She wanted to go find T.I. Jada pulled out her phone when she noticed Kierra on her phone.

> *I want to see Cascade before we leave.*
> *Yes, it the place T.I. filmed ATL.*
> *See where he stays so we can swing by his house, too.*

Kierra looked up from her phone, "Did you really have to text me that? We are sitting right next to each other. You could have said that."

"Well, you were on your phone. I didn't want to distract you."
Jada laughed, "Let me call and see how Bryson is doing. I haven't heard
from him in a few days."

Chapter Twenty-One

Richard felt so discouraged but he was not defeated. He didn't understand why he was having so many disappointments lately. He was feeling so alone. He wanted to call Brittany to see how she was doing. He knew she had probably seen the news and seen that Sean had met his fate. Richard wanted so badly to call her and let her know he was okay. Richard thought about the last time they had talked. Brittany let him know that she was glad she met him when he had retired his jersey. She was in loved with the man he had become and she would not have given Richie Rich the time of day. Brittany told him that she was afraid of people who sold drugs. She let him know that her grandmother always told her to be mindful of how you treat people and never entertain people that misused people for their own good. Brittany saw the best in Richard but the worse in Richie Rich. He just didn't know how he would let her know that he wasn't behind the murders. In just a short time Brittany was showing him the way to surrender his heart. His emotions were involved. Richard didn't even feel that way with Leslie. He had shared things with his past that he hadn't shared with anyone else.

Richard sat and was thinking about how he was going to love Brittany with all of his heart if she allowed him to. He struggled with where he thought he stood in Brittany' life. Richard wasn't even thinking about the money he had stashed in the wall that Brittany found. He had plenty more of where that came from. He smiled when he received the first text in a long while. He was impressed with her sexiness. Richard could not get the image of Brittany in the green chiffon dress out of his head. Richard was going to call her soon. He just needed to know what he was going to say. He just was not ready for any questions that Brittany may have had about Sean, Danitra, and Bryson. He thought back on the night from a few days ago.

When he had entered Sean's home and Sean led him to the safe Richard realized he didn't carefully plan that out. All his life he had planned things carefully. He had only found himself in an uncompromisable situation twice in his entire life. It was two times too many for him. Each time he hadn't planned things carefully ran him the risk of losing his life. The first time he and Sean crossed each other's paths and the next time was with Bryson. Going to visit Brittany he didn't expect to be put in a sticky situation. Sean had emptied his safe and the money was stacked up on the kitchen table.

Richard was thinking about how he was going to get out of there with the money. He wanted to send Danitra after a bag but he knew she was just as hard as Sean if not harder. She was not going to just go get a bag and come back. Richard didn't want to do a much of moving. Although he had Nina with him he knew if he made the wrong move Bryson and Sean would have the upper hand. Richard text Keith. He told him his location and told him not to come in the police cruiser that would bring too much attention. Richard let him know the back door would be open and it was safe for him to enter.

Keith arrived all alone. He walked right in the kitchen area. Richard was standing up against the sink and his hostages were just sitting at the kitchen table. Keith looked at the stacks of money on the table and ignored their angry faces. Richard brought his cousin up to date. Keith asked Bryson where he had put Leslie's body. Bryson didn't answer. Sean just looked very stern. Sean already knew this was not about to end well for them. He knew Richard loved Leslie. He wasn't sure if Richard was holding a grudge against him or was his just angry about the fact she had lost her life. Leslie was simply a casualty of the game. The queen was no longer interested in protecting here king, she was ready to switch teams and she did.

Sean didn't have all the details but he knew he would not be around to tell this story. Danitra stood up, "Look if I tell you where she is, would you let me out of here?"

Keith looked at Richard. He thought Richard was going to respond. He didn't. Keith looked at Danitra, "Sure. You start talking and I'll have some second thoughts. Why fit in with these losers by not saying anything when you were born to stand out?"

As Danitra stood up she walked over to the door, "She's over there under the barbecue pit."

Richard and Keith both looked out of the window. The barbecue was placed over a fresh thing of dirt on the side of the yard. As they were standing there looking at Leslie's grave site. Bryson figured it would be a good time for him to make his escape. He stood and ran towards the front door. Richard gave chase but Bryson was too quick. He was out the front door and down the street. The people who didn't listen to the police orders were back on the street. Richard was not about to put himself in a predicament to jeopardize his freedom. He would find Bryson in due time.

Richard headed back towards the kitchen. Keith turned to his cousin, "He got away didn't he." Richard didn't even answer his question. Keith put the silencer on his gun. Danitra and Sean died in their kitchen. Keith found a trash bag under the sink and placed the money it. While under the sink Keith found drug paraphernalia under the sink. Keith grabbed all the items he found. He left two stacks of money along with the digital scales, vials, and small zipper storage bags on the kitchen table.

While Keith was in the kitchen creating the crime scene, Richard was digging the dirt up where the barbecue pit once was placed. He was trying to be careful with the shovel. He didn't want to bring any more damage to Leslie's body. Keith was on his way out the door. He couldn't believe what he witnessing his cousin was doing.

Keith called his hot head friend. His friend showed right up. Michael couldn't believe what he saw although he had seen much worse. Michael owed Keith a favor. Michael let Keith know he would ever be in debt to him when he saved his little brother's life.

Michael's younger brother claim to fame were robberies. Keith was affiliated with a lot of street guys due to his relationship with Richard. One night Keith was having a drink with a few players. Michael's brother entered the establishment with a few of his friends. He got away but there was a price on his head. Let's just say Keith was able to keep Michael's brother alive. Michael told Keith to move Danitra's body out there near Leslie's. He helped him and told him to call it in.

The dispatcher dispatched about a disturbance. Michael let the dispatcher know he was in the area with a friend. So many police were busy throughout the city due to the verdict being released in the officer shooting. Different departments were just working together in support of one another. Michael had it all planned out. He was going to say he and Keith were sitting chatting when got the called. Keith followed him to the scene. That would explain why Keith DNA was at the crime scene if one had taking place. Keith broke Michael off three stacks and sent Richard on his way.

Richard knew he would never be able to tell or explain the details of that event with Brittany. It was killing him softly as he was trying to figure out his plan to move forward. He figured he would let it go. He pictured himself telling Brittany that there was a box and in that box, he had put Richie Rich. Richard was throwing that box in the Mississippi and if she wanted any information out of that box she would have to go and get it herself.

Richard placed the call he had been avoiding to make. He heard her saying hello and realized just how much he was missing her, "I would like to see you. Can you come over?"

Brittany smiled. She had been waiting for him to call her, "Yes, I will be there."

"Okay. I will see you then." Richard was about to hang up.

Brittany called out, "Richard."

A part of him didn't want to answer. He was afraid of what she made had asked him.

"Yes," he answered afraid of what may come next.

"We are going to leave everything and everyone in the past." Brittany wanted him to know that she was looking towards their future. She didn't want to know any more information about his past life. She looked at Danitra and Sean's death as the last chapter of Richard's street life. That was Brittany's way of ensuring him that he didn't have to open the book of Richie Rich anymore.

Brittany arrived at his place at seven o'clock sharp. When he opened the door to let her in Richard pictured her in that green chiffon dress. Richard looked right pass the green Adidas tracksuit she wearing. He was caught up in her physical attraction. That night he satisfied her physically and mentally. He made love to her that feed her mind and her soul.

Jarvis watched as the familiar face who can't place embraced the love of his life. He was about to go and talk to Brittany about their son. When he reached her house and was about to get out of his mother's car, he saw her coming out. She was smiling very hard and he hadn't seen her smile like that in a long time. Brittany appeared to be in a rush. Jada had come to the door to say something to her about Kierra and Check 'N Go. Brittany told her that she would call her when she made it to her destination. Jarvis decided to follow her to find out what was bringing the smile to her face that he hadn't seen to his release.

Chapter Twenty-Two

Hot topics flashed on the screen as Wendy Raquel, the former radio personality turned television host sat in the burgundy plush chair. She hosted a nationally syndicated television talk show. Jada sat down glued to the television when she saw a picture of Brittany in the green chiffon dress with the faux diamond brooch.

Wendy spoke, "Clap if you know who this is." There was a brief moment of silence. No one knew who Brittany was but Jada. She wasn't in the audience so no one heard her clap. Wendy continued being the gossip guru she was, "I thought I would have heard at least a few claps." Wendy laughed, "This girl pictured here as over a million followers on her blog titled *Tea with Brittany*. Okay moving on, let me tell you who she is. Now clap if you know this guy." A picture of Brittany's brother followed when hers came off the screen. The crowd went wild. Wendy continued, "We all know him as the friend that was with Mitchell Crawford when he was killed by the police." The audience clapped. Brittany's picture displayed again, "This is his sister, Brittany Gates." The audience was in awe. They screamed, "Oh," and hadn't heard the entire story of why she was a hot topic. Wendy continued, "Well, we all know and love our friend Rickey Smiley. A few weeks ago she and her friends attended his charity event. One of her close friends designed the dressed photographed here. Okay, that's so off the topic. Let me focus. She is someone to be on the lookout for. Brittany Gates is making a name for herself. I think if she rides the wave of that Mitchell Crawford story she may have a book deal in the works. Hold on, you know my staff did some investigation. Now she and her friends worked at a check cashing place. Guess what happened to the check cashing place?"

The audience in unison screamed out, "What?"

Wendy continued, "It just so happened to be located in Ferguson and during the unrest it was one of the buildings that burned down."

The audience went wild, "Wow!"

"You think we should invite Brittany to the show?" Wendy asked her audience and again they went wild. They applauded while Wendy made several expressions. They stopped clapping, "Brittany if you are watching give my producers a call we would love to talk to you about your blog." Wendy winked her eye and the network took a commercial break.

Jada sat there in shocked. She couldn't believe her dress had made it all the way to the Wendy Raquel show. She was certain that things for the *Pink Legacy Boutique* were going to take off. She thought about all the boutique owners and none of them had not been on national television. Jada grabbed her cellphone she had to let Brittany know that Wendy Raquel knew who she was and there were no limits to their dreams. Jada knew Brittany was with Richard but she didn't care. This phone call was very important.

Jada waited on Brittany to answer her phone. Brittany saw that Jada had called. She was going to call her back. She was on the phone with her brother. He was letting her know that he, Demeasha, and the baby were headed to Phoenix. Brandon let Brittany know he needed a new environment. The media and the police were not letting him rest. The police harassed him every opportunity that they had. He didn't understand why. Each arrest was publicized on the local news station. Brandon called his mother and let her know he needed a change. He apologized to Pat for all the pain he ever caused. His mother accepted his apology and let him know she was going to welcome him and his family into her home. Brandon and his family were leaving the first thing in the morning.

Brittany wanted to be upset with her mother. She and Jarvis had been displaced due to the fire at their family home. Not once did she open up her home to Brittany and Jarvis. Brittany blew it off. She let Brandon know that she and Jarvis would be by to see them off. While Brittany was on the phone with her brother Brandon she began to get several phone calls. Her aunt Alexis called along with Crystal, Kierra and Jada had even called her back to back. She let Brandon know she would be over as soon as she picked Jarvis up.

Brittany had to call everyone back. She called Jada first. Jada was filled with excitement. She could feel it through the phone. Brittany could not believe what Jada was saying. She didn't believe that Wendy Raquel thought she was that important to have her as a hot topic. Brittany thought about not having the typical life while growing up. She has always felt as though negativity had dominated her life and let her powerless. Brittany thought about every situation she had been faced with had worked against her. As she listened to her longtime friend Jada she realized that there were no limits to what she could achieve. She told Jada that her mother turned her own to fashion from all things she had shoplifted and her fashions were about to be exposed to the world due to her famous friend.

When Brittany ended the call with Jada she realized why everyone was calling her. She was glad she let Jada know to call Crystal and Kierra. She was going to get her son so they could say their goodbyes to her brother Brandon before he and his family left for Phoenix.

Richard sat and watched Brittany as she had talked to her brother and then to her friend. He was just satisfied with her presence. He just wanted to love her. Richard thought about the day he met her at church. From everyone, he encountered that day Brittany was the only one who had a vibe that filled him with joy. When he saw her at Chili's he knew it was not just a mere coincidence.

That morning he was getting ready for church he was listening to Joel Olsten. During the sermon, he preached about God strategically placing the people you need in your life. Richard had turned his life around and became a humble servant of the most high. He felt that Brittany was his reward for his service here on earth.

Brittany let Richard know she would back. She was going to pick up her son and meet with her brother. Brittany asked him was he ready to me her first true love. He let her know he wanted to meet everyone that was special to her. Brittany left to out to pick up her offspring.

Brittany got a rude awakening when she made it to Jarvis's parents' home. He greeted her at the door. Jarvis stood in the door. It was obvious he was not going to let her in.

"How may I help you?" Jarvis was speaking with a broken heart. He avoided looking in her eyes. He couldn't deny he was still in love.

"Hey, Jarvis. I was coming to pick up my baby so he can see Brandon and his family before they leave." She sensed a little animosity from Jarvis but she ignored it, "You know Brandon is having a hard time ever since he witnessed the murder of Mitchell Crawford. Pat agreed that he needed a change. So they are leaving in the morning."

Jarvis stood there for a minute. He had been practicing a speech he was going to give to Brittany the moment she called or showed up. Brittany was standing there waiting for him to respond or at least let her in.

Jarvis finally spoke, "He has been getting along very well without you in his life. You made the choice to run along and do you. You have replaced me so we are going to replace you. I guess someone else's tender touch makes you smile. You couldn't forgive me for my mistake. It's all good, though. We good. Why don't you go ahead and bounce? We both will be are just fine and with you out of our life may be best." Jarvis slammed the door.

Epilogue

Brittany Gates was running, as though she was trying to outdo Usain Bolt, through the terminal of Lambert-St. Louis International Airport with her son Jarvis in tow. She was moving swiftly and Jarvis was keeping up with her as if she were a Kardashian not missing a beat. She could overhear on the airport's intercom, as she got closer to the gate, "C19, last call for flight 5743 to Phoenix," being dispatched for the third time. Brittany was so disgusted with herself that she had sat at the wrong gate for over an hour and a half. She was clinging to their boarding pass as if it was their last supper. When she finally made it to the correct destination, the entire area was empty. There were no patrons waiting to board the next plane. This was unusual. Once an airplane had been boarded and the area was clear; a group of new people would flock to the area to await their time for the next plane that would soon be approaching. All she knew and could remember was her mother telling her that the gate closed ten minutes before the flight departed. The workers need to prepare for take-off. She was there with four minutes to spare. With the entire city looking for her, she knew she couldn't stay in St. Louis one second longer. Missing this flight was not an option for her. When she arrived at gate C19 she immediately handed off each boarding pass to be scanned.

Breathing heavily, Brittany looked down at her son, "Jarvis, you are going to be a track star, just like I was when I was in school, I see!" Brittany reminisced about her high school days. She rarely even ran these days. She couldn't remember the last time she even ran for exercise.

184

She pulled her red St. Louis Cardinals baseball cap tightly over her eyes and looked down at Jarvis as they began to walk through the jet bridge to board the aircraft. Jarvis tugged at his mother shirt to get her attention. She briefly turned around and caught a glimpse of her picture plastered on the television that was hoisted on the wall, near the Chili's restaurant which was directly across from her boarding gate. The airline worker who had just scanned her boarding pass took a glimpse at Brittany and turned her attention back towards the television.

Brittany thought to herself, *"How could I be wanted for kidnapping my own son? I walked in that school and signed him out."*

The school didn't question her when she arrived to pick him up. Jarvis was so happy to see his mom. She told the office a story about a doctor's appointment his grandmother forgot about and she was there to take him to the doctor. It was only until later that they realized his grandmother, Jarvis's mom, had completed the enrollment. Brittany Gates was nowhere on his paperwork.

The news reporter was starting their reports off with the good news that a local was getting national exposure. The good news shifted to the bad news. Brittany was wanted for kidnapping Jarvis from his private school.

Brittany took her seat and placed her headphones in. She let the soothing sounds of Mary J. Blige relax her. She was with her everything. It was because of Jarvis, Jr. she had the sunshine on the cloudiest of days.

When she went to the airport to see Brandon off she purchased two tickets. Brandon was looking for his nephew. Brittany conjured up a quick lie. She told him he was gone when she got there and she would have missed him if she would have waited for him to get back. Brittany didn't' want to tell him how Jarvis had played her. He had enough problems he was dealing with.

185

That night she stopped by Richard's to let him know she was going to see her mother. Richard let her know if she were gone too long he would be in Phoenix looking for here. She kissed him goodbye.

Brittany made it to her house. She found Jada working on *Pink Legacy Boutique* stuff. Brittany sat down beside her.

"I went by Jarvis's parents' house to pick up my son and Jarvis basically told me I would never see my son again. So in the morning I will be going to get him from school. I have already purchased our plane tickets to go see my mom. I'm going to go out there until I can figure some things out." Brittany began to cry. Jada held her and let her know that she understood.

Jada let her know that was a good idea and filled her in on the latest bit of information she had. She let her know their previous employer had reached out to Kierra. They were impressed with what she was doing with her Diamond in the Ruff organization. They offered her a top position to be over all the Check 'N Go's in the Metropolitan area of St. Louis. Kierra agreed. Each one of them was offered their job back but they all would have to work at different locations.

Brittany looked down at her phone. She read Richard's text message.

> *Safe travels. I have a very good lawyer that will take care of all this. I will be headed out to meet with you and your loved ones in a few days.*

Brittany smiled. She became frustrated when her phone started to vibrate she just wanted to relax. She looked down and didn't recognize the number. She answered.

"Hello, Brittany. This is Damon Antal. I'm a producer here at the OWN network."

Teresa Seals

READING GROUP GUIDE

Discussion Questions

1. How would you explain Pat's, Brittany's mother, relationship with her daughter?
2. How would you have handled imperative information with a close friend if you were Brittany?
3. Describe the relationship between Jarvis and Brittany. Compare it to Richard and Brittany's relationship.
4. Richard shared information about his former life with Brittany. Would you have stuck around with him?
5. Do you think Brittany had the better them than me when it came to the death of her brother's friend? Explain your thoughts in details with your group.
6. How would you describe the overall friendship of Brittany, Jada, Kierra and Crystal? How loyal were they to each other? Can you compare your loyalty to a friend?
7. Kierra wanted to contact the authorities about Bryson. Explain how you would have handled the Bryson situation.
8. Describe your overall feelings about No Limit. Do you like the way it ended? Why or Why not?

AVAILABLE NOW

COMING SUMMER 2017

AN EXCERPT FROM THE YOUNG AND THE RECKLESS

CHAPTER 1

"This is my last time asking yo ass!" The tall masked man spoke with authority. "You need to open this safe right now or its lights out for you, brah!" The masked man barked his demands as he pointed the black Smith and Wesson towards the top of Xavier's head. The masked man looked down on Xavier and could see the fear in his eyes as he kneeled on the side of his king size bed in front of a custom made safe. Xavier looked towards the masked man and tried to avoid making eye contact with him. Xavier didn't know how this would end. The merciless look in the eyes of the man that was hoisted over him gave him a sinister feeling. He feared his wife waking up to two unknown individuals standing in their bedroom, demanding he open a safe that she didn't agree with being there in the first place. Xavier was wrapping his mind around the situation and began to realize that this was not about to end well for him and his wife. He glanced at the clock that sat on top of the safe that was designed to look as if it were a very expensive nightstand. Only on the surface, the African Blackwood revealed its elegance. Hand engraved floral work were along the edges and on the top were four small lions engraved in each corner. The African Blackwood covered up a ten cubic feet electronic safe that contained a half a million dollars. In their bedroom were two identical nightstands. One you could actually open the front and utilize. The door and handle were an imposter on the other nightstand. It only opened from the top. As soon as it opened the keypad was there waiting for you to enter the magic four-digit code.

The time was 3:14. When he noticed the time, he knew Nevaeh would be coming in their room in under fifteen minutes, to climb in their bed and Cinque would be sure to follow. At the age of six, Nevaeh still needed to be tricked to sleep in her bed. She hadn't learned to make it through the night. Like clockwork she would show up at 3:29. Xavier thought it was very ironic that she was born March

29th and she came into their bedroom every day at that time. Cinque would be right behind her as if he knew that he needed to cherish ever moment he had with his mother and father. He smiled in amazement thinking about how his ten-year-old son still craved for his attention as if he were three. His smile quickly became a frown as he knew he needed to end this situation soon. Xavier made the decision to plead his case, "Look, man, my kids are in the other room and I don't want any problems. For the last time, that's my brother safe, I don't know the combination." He looked up, avoiding making direct eye contact, to see if the guy was about to be sympathetic. When he noticed there was no change in the man's disposition, he continued, "Look my man; I can get the combination to the safe. Just give me some time."

　　　　With tears rolling down his face, Xavier kept his eyes on the man who had a 38 revolver pointed at his wife's head as she slept peacefully. Being the big brother trying to help the little brother, he allowed him to stash his illegal money in his home. The custom made safe depicted an overprice nightstand that he knew that his little brother had to be running his mouth about. He knew his brother like to boast. It was a bad characteristic that he had had. He never imagined that his little brother's boasting and bragging would lead him to this life or death moment. Xavier said a silent prayer hoping that his wife would not wake up and be startled by what was taken place in their bedroom. Before Xavier could respond the loud gunshot sent a ringing through his ears and a chill shook his soul. His tears stopped and eyes became filled with rage. At that moment Xavier decided whether he should find a piece of paper that had the combination that his brother had written down or rather he was ready to go with his wife. He looked at the guy that was standing over him. He noticed that he appeared just as devastated as he was. He had loosened his grip on the gun just enough that Xavier fixated his eyes on the familiar image engraved on the handle of this black and army green smith and Wesson 9mm. Before he could make a decision or say a word his body failed to the ground.

The sound of the phone ringing startled Cinque. Three days in a row he had dreamed about his parent's murder. It had been seven years and the crime had yet to be solved. He smiled as he watched Star's name and picture come across the screen. He smiled admiring her moisturized mocha complexion, "Hello." The birthmark that flowed from her hairline onto her forehead didn't intercede with her beauty. He always thought it was quite unique. Star thought it was hideous and always hid it with a baseball cap or bangs.

"Hey, Cinque this is Star. Well of course you know it is me, my name is programmed in your phone. I hate to disappoint you, but I'm not having such a good idea about this. I was a little excited thinking about this road trip but my gut feeling is telling me that this is not going to end well." Star took her time as she chose her words carefully. "I know you said we could shop. Lord knows I need some new clothes but." She paused and took a deep breath, "I really can't explain it but something does not sit right with me about this trip."

"Come on Star. You can't do this to me. You do not have to worry about anything. I am not going to put you in a compromising situation. I just figured we can catch up on old times and get to know one another all over again. I promise I will not try anything." Cinque was glad his phone had ranged and interrupted the nightmare that had haunted him ever since he was 10 years old. He wanted some answers and he thought at least once he would see some sort of sign that would reveal the people who he sought to give the ultimate payback. If it was there, he hadn't noticed it in seven years but he was not about to give up.

"Cinque, I am not worried about you trying anything. I've been bullying you since we were five years old. Do you think things changed just because of us being older?" Star laughed.

"Girl, a lot has changed. You seem to be a bit confused. Let me get you hip real quick. We not five and I'm on big boy status now. I don't get bullied. I am the bully. So go ahead and get ready and I'll be there around six in the morning. And you can drop the Cin and just call me Que." Cinque hung up the phone before Star could change her mind.

Cinque looked at the time on his cell phone. He had six hours. He packed an overnight bag so Star would think they would be actually spending the night in Chicago. He knew if they were on the road by seven, they would make it to their destination by twelve. His plan was to stop and get something to eat at the Frontera Grill, check in to the hotel, shop, pick up his package, rest for about three hours, get back on the road and head back home.

Cinque was making his way towards Star's house. He hadn't been on the side of the town since he was 10 years old. Running into Star a few weeks back had brought him back to his roots. When he came back to the neighborhood the first time to meet Star was the first night that the nightmares resurfaced. Now the last two weeks that gruesome image from the worse night of his life wouldn't leave his mind.

As he was about to turn down his old street, he thought he was reliving his past. Police cars and the ambulance had the street blocked. He was curious to know what was going on this early in the morning. He parked his car on the corner, got out the car and made his way down the street. Cinque saw a familiar face. He noticed Star's mother just screaming and hollering. It was 6 am and people were out parleying as if it were noon. Some individuals had on clothes like they were headed to work while others were draped in pajamas and housecoats. Cinque could see nothing had changed. Drama bought everyone on the block out the house. He rushed over to Star's mother and she immediately grabbed him and held on tight. He began to cry with her not even know what they were crying for. She knew exactly who he was.

Cinque was a spitting image of a dad Xavier and his uncle Hot Rod. Patty admired his rich brown skin, the stern in which their eyes seem to always have and the broad protruding nose that made them appear very serious. He even had the precise lined deep black hair that was neatly trimmed and never out of place. He wondered did she even know who he was. He had been by there lately but he never ran into her. He honestly thought that she had run off because she had dreams of being a Hollywood star. Star's mother hadn't uttered a simple word. He had the look of confusion on his face as he was trying to figure out what was going on. She had her head buried in his chest. With her in his arms, he stepped back and looked at the crowd. As he stood near the front of the ambulance, he noticed that the paramedics had the back doors open to the ambulance. He could tell they were working on someone and he needed to know who, but his fears had taken over him. He kept scanning the crowd and growing curiously to know who was in the ambulance. He began to take baby steps as he held on to Patty, easing them to the back of the ambulance. As he moved inch by inch, Cinque was surveying the crowd to see if he could see Star. As they reached the door of the ambulance, he had a sigh of relief. Star had surfaced from the ambulance.

Star hopped down off the back of the ambulance and headed over to Cinque and shook her head. "Ma, are you going to ride in the ambulance with Nanna?" Star stood there waiting on her mother's response with the ugliest attitude.

Cinque was so glad to see her. Just seeing her gave him a sense of relief. He let go of Star's mother and held on to Star. He looked up to the sky, "Thank you!"

Star looked at Cinque strangely and laughed, "Boy, what's wrong with you? And I know you didn't just thank God!?"

"I actually thought something had happened to you. When I saw your mother standing here all alone crying. I got nervous. I damn near panicked. You hear me." Cinque smirked.

"As you can see, nothing has happened to me. My grandmother fell and hit her head. She claimed she lost balance when she got out the bed. I noticed the blood at the top of her head and called 911. Patty out here doing too much and the paramedics had to call for backup. They just let her out of the police car!" Star looked at her mother was disgust.

"I see she hasn't changed. Always got to be dramatic." Cinque looked at Patty.

"We'll Cinque, I am not going to be able to take this road trip. So you can go ahead, I'm about to go to this hospital with my Nanna and make sure everything's okay with her." Star said to Cinque.

"Que! How many times I have to tell you that." He smiled, "Let me make this phone call and I can follow you all to the hospital." Cinque kissed Star on her forehead and walked back to his car.

The police cleared the traffic and the people start to disperse. Cinque picked up the phone and called his little sister as he got in his car so that he could be ready to pull off behind the ambulance. The ambulance drove through the city streets in silence and flashing lights. Cinque followed at a steady pace.

Cinque grabbed his phone from his waist to call his sister. When he noticed she answered the phone, he began to speak, "Nevaeh, listen." He instructed, "I need you to do me a huge favor and you cannot say, no."

Nevaeh rolled her eyes, "What is it now?"

"Look I'm about to head to this hospital with Star. I don't know how long I am going to be up here and I got to be at that place for Unc. You know that little thing you did before for me when I threw that kickback and couldn't go myself." He didn't wait for her to answer, "I need you to do it again. One more time for the one time, please."

"That's all? I thought you wanted something major. Like, be Carlos girlfriend again. I'm game. But, let me tell you this now, it is going to cost you more. What time you want me to leave?"

Cinque paused. He was kind of hesitant. He didn't know how she was going to respond when he said right now.

"Hello. Did you hear me, boy?" Nevaeh grew a tad bit frustrated.

"Right now," Cinque spoke softly.

"Right now! You got to be kidding me. This is really going to cost you more. Last minute. I don't even know if I could get someone to ride with me on such a short notice.' Nevaeh shook her head.

"Call Paradise." Cinque smiled waiting on Nevaeh to respond.

"Yeah, I will call her and you bet not ignore her call when she calls you. Que I'm about to call Paradise. One!" Nevaeh pressed end.

Before she could get to Paradise's name on her phone, Big Bro came across her screen. She started to press ignore send him so the voicemail but she knew he called right back.

"What now?" Nevaeh waited on what he had to say.

"Dude expecting you at four. So look here, call me when you are getting on the highway, call me as soon as you get to Bloomington, call me as soon as you get off I-55, call me when you pull up to the spot, call me when you leave the spot, call me when you are getting back on I-55, Call me again when you reach Bloomington.". Got that?"

Nevaeh interrupted, "Dude I know. Same as before. One!"

He hated when she said that. Ever since she seen the movie *Belly* and DMX would say it when he hung up the phone, she thought was just the greatest thing. She said that was better than saying the word bye. One day she told him bye meant gone forever and she hated the thought of forever.

Nevaeh had picked up Paradise hit the highway and may her phone calls as instructed. When she made her last phone call, it would be the phone call that Cinque did not want to hear. Nevaeh looked in the rearview mirror and watched the flashing lights as she made her phone call.

"Hey Que, I just want you to know, we just got pulled over. The cop just took my license I walked back to his car. So now we just sitting here waiting."

"Did you do the speed limit and use your signals like I told you? He spoke calm and firm.

He pulled me over and said the police are looking for a black Ford Escape that wanted for questioning in some shooting. You know I haven't shot anyone. I should be cool, but I will call you back in a second." Nevaeh pressed end and deleted her incoming and outgoing call log. Nevaeh and Paradise both looked in their rearview mirrors. They sit in silence as they watch more police cruisers pull up.

Teresa Seals

The Young and the Reckless

Teresa Seals